MW00985872

A WYNTERFELL ROMANCE BOOK ONE
For the Love of Hot Cocoa
STEPHANIE K CLEMENS

For the Love of Hot Cocoa

Stephanie K. Clemens

Book Cover by Blackstone Cover Designs

Check out my website www.stephaniekclemens.com

I want to dedicate this book to my inability to focus on another book, and my mom.

Content Information

This book is intended to be a Cozy Fantasy but that doesn't mean there aren't references or discussions of serious topics. These include prejudice/discrimination, child neglect (off page) and abduction.

Chapter One

ICELYN FROST—PURVEYOR OF ALL THINGS CHOCOLATE. Icelyn read the brand-new sign hanging over her brand-new shop. She loved how the swirl of the letters looked like tempered chocolate atop a perfectly iced cake, not to mention how the deep brown color shined next to the magenta-and-ivory striped awning. The tradesfolk who had worked to get her shop ready for the grand opening had outdone themselves. She might have been guilty of bribing them with both chocolate and non-chocolate baked goods, along with hot drinks. But who would blame her? She had a talent and she might as well use it to her advantage whenever she could.

"We did it, Ember. Just look at the sign, the shop. It's perfect, and it's ours." She looked down at her pet mini-dragon. Ember was looking especially good today. Her purple scales were extra shiny, perfect for the upcoming grand opening.

Ember let out a little puff of smoke, agreeing with Icelyn. She flapped her wings, causing her to hover just above the ground. It was Ember's favorite way to show excitement.

Icelyn flipped her unicorn-colored hair over her shoulder. The pinks, blues, purples, and silvers of her wavy hair cascaded down her back. Her hair was different, even for Wynterfell.

She could thank her mother for the shimmery uniqueness. Not everyone could claim a unicorn as a mother, but she could, even if she didn't really remember much about her, but what she did remember was really quite a story.

Her father, Jonathan Frost, met her mother, Astrea, during the Great Protection, when hunters were set on depleting the unicorn population, hunting them for the magic in their horns. To protect them, the castle's wizard turned all unicorns human.

One day Jonathan was walking in the forest and stumbled across Astrea. It was love at first sight, and it felt like a love of the ages. Until the day the wizard showed up at their door, offering a safe place for Astrea to be in her natural form.

Jonathan encouraged her to go, knowing how much she missed that life, even if it meant leaving him and their young daughter behind.

Icelyn shook the memories off, muttering to herself as she shifted her focus away from her past and towards her future. "What do you think, Ember? I hope we can be a part of all the winter festivities. Just imagine how many customers we will have if we take part in the entire holiday season." She clapped her hands together and twirled, Ember flying in circles around her. This was her dream come true. At least it would be, once it was successful.

"Icelyn Frost, this place is splendid." Holly Green squealed, throwing her arms around her best friend, nearly knocking the two of them to the ground. "I'm so happy for you."

Icelyn felt her friend shiver. "Let's get inside. It's absolutely frigid out here."

As she pulled out the heavy key, she took a deep breath. She slid it into the lock, and with half a twist, the door popped open. She stepped aside, letting Holly and Ember through. The café was a silvery grey color with pops of magenta, and the tables were a rich brown that reminded her of swirls of milk and dark chocolate. A cream-colored candle sat as the centerpiece of each table.

"Ember," Icelyn called; in seconds, her pet dragon was in front of her, flapping her wings. "Can you light the fireplace fire and the candles?"

Ember let out a puff of smoke before turning to do as asked. She hopped from one table to another, letting out a small flame to light each of the candles. It wasn't long before all the candles were lit, and the dragon was in front of the fire, blowing a solid stream of flame into the stone structure until the wood caught fire. Soon the room filled with warmth and a sense of coziness.

Instead of heading to one of the many tables in the room, Icelyn escorted her companions to the overstuffed teal sofas next to the fireplace. She hoped people looking to read a good book while enjoying a chocolate treat would enjoy this spot. It's why she had installed bookshelves and made sure all her favorite fairy tales were there.

"Have you shown your father your café? It's so cozy and so you. He must be very proud." Holly plopped down on the sofa, a mound of pillows surrounding her.

"Not yet. I want to have regular customers before I show it off. It's just such an enormous risk. I don't want to tell everyone in case it doesn't work out."

"You know better than to focus on your doubts. You have to manifest your success." Holly glared at Icelyn, folding her arms. "Now, stop biting your nails—you only do that when you let your fear of failure overwhelm you—and start focusing on how this place is your dream."

"I know, it's just . . ." Icelyn rolled her shoulders and pivoted to face the kitchen. "Just give me a moment, and I'll have peppermint hot cocoas for all of us." Icelyn pulled her hair back out of her face and into a ponytail.

"My favorite: peppermint hot cocoa and peppermint mochas. Sometimes that little extra kick is what I need in the morning."

"I was planning on entering my peppermint hot cocoa in the competition at the Snow Solstice Festival, but I'm not sure. I'm worried it's too basic and I need to come up with something more creative—unique, but with all the creamy goodness that makes you want another sip." Icelyn brought out two of her signature ceramic hand-warmer mugs and a bowl of warm oat milk for Ember on a tray.

"You worry too much. I've never tasted anything you've made and not wanted another sip or bite. In fact, I volunteer as your official taste-tester for all things leading up to the Snow Solstice Festival." Holly smiled and took a sip of her drink. "Seriously, what do you do to make everything so good? It's like you use magic."

"Love, everything is made with love. Which is its very own type of magic."

Chapter Two

"An ultimatum, my father, the king, gave me an ultimatum." Prince Colden Whittaker sprawled in the green velvet wingback chair, kicking his booted leg over the arm of the chair.

"His Highness has a tendency to get exactly what he wants. The real question is, what does he want from you this time?" Douglas asked.

Colden looked at the captain of the guard and his longtime friend. "It's more like, what doesn't he want? I don't mind taking on more responsibility; in fact, I long for it. But he's put me in charge of the Snow Solstice Festival, a frivolous task, instead of something with meaning. In addition, my father has insisted I find a spouse by the end of the festival."

"The festival is important to Wynterfell, especially to all the merchants. I wouldn't call it frivolous," Douglas scolded the prince. "And marriage might not be that bad. I wouldn't know though; I'm still living the single life."

Colden shifted his lanky frame until he was sitting upright, pushing his fingers through his black hair. "You're right, I'm acting like an entitled ass. This event is special to my father's people, some day my people, and I need to respect what matters to them."

"That was easier than I thought it would be. It's always nice when you not only listen to me but admit I'm right." Douglas laughed. "Let's go into town, find out what the townsfolk need this winter. You can make the Snow Solstice Festival the best the town has ever seen."

"You're right, that's exactly the attitude I need to take." Colden jumped from his seat, ready to start his new task with enthusiasm, ignoring the second part of the assignment from his father. He wasn't ready for the responsibility that came with a spouse—especially if the match wasn't fueled with love. Responsibility could only keep a marriage going for so long. "I have a better idea."

"You don't want to go to town?"

"I do, but I don't want to go as the prince. It's time for an incognito mission." Colden rubbed his hands together, the wheels turning in his head. "I want to learn what the village needs, and if they know it's me, everyone will be, well, polite. If this festival is going to make a difference, I don't need polite, I need to hear the truth."

Douglas stroked his red beard. "It's not a bad idea, but I think the townsfolk would rather see you involved as you. They want to know you care."

"Hmmm, something to think about, but for today I don't want to be noticed if I can help it." He grabbed his wool cloak.

"Like anyone could see you in that cloak and those boots and not know who you are," Douglas muttered.

"What did you say?" Colden asked from the doorway.

"Nothing, sir. Nothing at all."

With the shops along Main Street dusted with snow, the village of Wynterfell glistened in the sunlight. Every door was decked out with an evergreen wreath or trimmed with garland filled with red berries and pinecones. It was a picturesque sight to see as everyone geared up for the Snow Solstice Festival. Taking in all the decorations around him, Colden was reminded of the excitement the festival used to bring him, especially when he was a kid. It was a child's winter dream with competitions galore. His favorites were always the snow sculpture challenge and the snowball battle. His mother was always most excited about the ice skaters and the shop decorations, while his father loved the sled dragon races and the marketplace. He said the festival market was where he always felt closest to the people of Wynterfell. It gave him a chance to see what made the townsfolk happiest. Colden hadn't understood it as a child, but he was starting to see why it was so important to his father now, especially as he stood at the edge of downtown and could feel the energy all around him.

He sauntered down Main Street, looking into different shops along the way. He stopped in front of a pretty magenta awning. "Douglas, is this shop new? I don't think I recognize it." There was a small sign in the window that read baked goods.

"Oh-My-Gods! It's Prince Colden."

Startled, he turned towards the sound of a woman's voice. That was his first mistake.

The second was making eye contact with the petite blonde pointing at him. While she looked attractive in her icy-blue winter gown, she had completely undermined his ability to remain incognito.

"I knew it was you the moment I saw you. No one could mistake you for anyone other than the prince." The woman rushed over to him, words dropping out of her mouth one on top of the other, so fast it was almost impossible to distinguish what it was she was saying.

"You must be m . . ."

"Stacey, how dare you not tell me the prince is here, across the street from our little café?" A young man wearing a bright fuchsia coat followed behind the blonde.

"I didn't know he was out here, Dru." She stomped her foot with a huff. "How would I? I was inside with you until just a few moments ago."

Colden glanced back at Douglas, a look of sheer terror on his face. Douglas just shrugged, a lot of help he was. Colden turned back to the duo rushing towards him, plastering a princely smile on his face.

"You've found me out. I'm visiting town to get ideas for the upcoming festival. I must . . ." He turned to leave, but to no avail.

"The festival," shrieked Stacey. She jumped up and down, everything, including her curls, bouncing in unison. "Oh my, I have such ideas. Why don't we grab a bite, and I can tell you all of them?" Stacey grabbed his arm, completely disregarding his status.

"Stacey, do not distract the prince with your blathering. If he wanted your ideas, I'm sure he would have asked," Dru said, taking Colden by the other arm. "I'm sure you aren't interested in the ideas of a frivolous girl. I, however, have been thinking about the festival for ages, and have made a list of improvements from last year."

Colden's eyes darted wildly as they dragged him away from the pretty magenta awning towards Mother Maude's Tea and Coffee House. For a brief moment his eyes met Douglas's, who threw his head back, laughing. It was apparent Colden was not getting any assistance from that corner.

He stopped, extricating himself from the couple, then they stopped. "Actually, I was headed to that shop there," he said, pointing to the place they had pulled him away from.

Stacey gasped. Dru shook his head.

"You do not want to go there. Mother Maude's is much better," Stacey said as she grabbed the prince by the arm and pulled Colden away from the pretty shop, towards the tea and coffee house. Which did not look nearly as inviting as . . . He looked behind him to catch the shop name, but he only managed to see the last few words . . . PURVEYOR OF ALL THINGS CHOCOLATE.

Chapter Three

"They did it again. They escorted another potential customer away from my café. Holly, how am I going to succeed if Dru and Stacey steal every single person that comes near here?" Icelyn's head fell to the counter.

She was sick of those two stealing any guests that would pay attention to her. Ember let out a puff of smoke. Icelyn absently petted Ember's head in response.

"Don't despair, I've got ideas brewing in my noggin. Granted, it would be much easier if you let me stoop to their level. But I know you won't, so I'm trying to come up with some sneaky ideas that you won't find morally repugnant." Holly flipped her thick red braid over her shoulder. It fell past her waist, all the way down to her thigh. Holly leaned onto the counter next to Icelyn, thrumming her fingers as she plotted.

"We could—wait, no, you would never approve. How about—no, that's no good either. I know—"

The bell above the door tinkled, letting Icelyn know someone was in her shop.

Wait, someone just walked through the door!

She had a customer! Her head popped up; her bright smile seemed to light up the entire room. Walking towards her was a brawny, red-haired lumberjack of a man, with a full beard completing the look.

"Welcome to my café, what can I get for you today?" Icelyn stumbled over herself in her attempt to welcome the first person Stacey and Dru hadn't swept away. "Oh my gods, I'm so sorry. Please, have a seat."

The man chuckled and grabbed a chair at one of her dainty tables. He looked so out of place she almost started to laugh, but she stopped herself because she didn't want to be rude. Once she started laughing, there was no way she was going to be able to stop. It had been one of those days. Right now, she was only holding on by a thread, one that was fraying.

"I couldn't resist stopping, your shop front is so inviting. And the name, purveyor of all things chocolate—it's like you predicted all my wants and desires without ever meeting me." The man looked around her tiny café, eyes pausing on Holly briefly before returning to Icelyn.

"I'm Icelyn Frost and I know a thing or two about loving chocolate. What are you looking for today? Cake, brownies, candies, hot beverages, or"—she paused for effect— "something without chocolate."

She glanced back at Holly, who was staring at the lumberjack, jaw slack. Holly must have felt Icelyn looking at her because she jerked her head towards their guest and made eye contact with Icelyn, mouthing *Oh-my-gods. Yummy!*

Icelyn bit back a giggle before turning back to her only customer, the only customer she had had since her store opened a few days ago. She needed him to love her place, it was imperative. She heard Ember flapping behind her.

"And who is this little cutie?" the man asked.

"Oh, that's Ember." Icelyn glared at Ember. "I'm sorry. I can take her to the back."

"Don't do that on my account," he said as Ember snuggled up against him. He bent over and picked up the dragon, setting her on his lap.

"Anything sound good?" she asked with a smile.

"Everything sounds fantastic; Colden is going to be so mad those two piranhas hijacked him. I know he's not going to get to try anything half as good as I am." He took a deep breath. "I don't think I've ever been anywhere that's smelled this good."

"Did you say Colden, as in *Prince* Colden?" Icelyn stared in disbelief.

"I did."

"If he's here, in town, and you're with him, you must be Sir Douglas Fir, his royal guard." She stood there fidgeting, shocked by the man in front of her.

"I am."

"Shouldn't you be with him? I mean—I'm sorry, I shouldn't question how you go about doing your job. It's just Stacey and Dru are so . . ." Icelyn trailed off, realizing she was babbling and didn't have anything nice to say about her competition, and step-siblings.

She remembered how her unicorn mother left to live out her life as the gods intended, as a beautiful unicorn, leaving Jonathan Frost all alone with their young daughter. At a loss, he remarried a local, Maude Mavern of Mother Maude's Tea and Coffee House. Icelyn had been excited, especially since not only did she get a new mother, but she also got a brother and a sister and, to top it off, they were twins. But Drusillo and Anastasia, better known around Wynterfell as Dru and Stacey, were awful to her, as was their mother, Maude. Unfortunately, Icelyn's father travelled so much for work he never understood why Icelyn was so unhappy.

"Awful, annoying, obnoxious," Douglas said.

"What?" Icelyn shook her head to bring herself back to the present.

"I was just attempting to finish your sentence, 'Stacey and Dru are so'—I suggested awful, annoying, and obnoxious."

"Haha, you've described their personalities spot on," Holly chimed in, leaving her safe space behind the counter. "Icelyn will not do anything about them escorting every single potential customer away from here. But it's just going to continue to happen unless someone does something about it. By the way, I'm Holly." She held her hand out to Douglas.

"Nice to meet you, Holly." He raised her hand to his lips, then winked, before letting it go.

"Aren't you absolutely swoon worthy?" Holly winked back before sitting next to Douglas.

Icelyn rolled her eyes. Holly was an impetuous flirt, falling in and out of love as often as a normal person changed their undergarments. Although, they were pretty cute with their coordinating red hair.

"Would you like a sampler of what I have here? It's on the house," Icelyn said.

"Icelyn," Holly hissed with a meaningful look.

She knew Holly was telling her to charge Douglas, that he was the only customer that had ventured into her café since she opened and she couldn't afford to give away anything. But a connection like this could change everything, and if free chocolate helped establish a connection, it would be well worth it.

"I would love a sampler plate and something to drink. But I can pay. The prince values my service, and I'm compensated accordingly," Douglas said.

"I guess I'll have to charge you then." Icelyn smiled, then turned to make her way to the back. She put a pot on the stove to heat the oat milk for her peppermint hot cocoas. She plated a piece of her chocolate ganache cake with a dollop of whipped cream, a slice of chocolate Solstice log filled with whiskey cream frosting and covered with chocolate bark; next to that she added a mini peppermint-mocha cupcake, and finished the plate off with one of her non-chocolate specialties, a pumpkin spice cupcake filled with apples sautéed in a cinnamon bourbon and topped with cream cheese frosting. It was a dessert plate fit for a king, or at the very least the prince's captain of the guard.

She carefully balanced three mugs of cocoa and the dessert plate on her serving tray and brought it out front. She set everything on the table in front of Douglas and Holly with a flourish.

"Look at this feast of sweets. I don't think I've ever seen so many delectable-looking desserts in one place. Are they as good as they look?" Douglas asked.

"Better," Holly and Icelyn responded in unison.

"Gods, I hope I didn't just drool thinking about trying these. That would be embarrassing, but could anyone blame me?" Douglas wiped his mouth. "So, what do I have in front of me?"

Icelyn rattled off each dessert, giving Douglas and Holly a chance to take a bite of each one. She finished by telling them about the cocoa and waited for a response from at least one of them. She continued to wait as they went back for one bite after another. It wasn't until the plate was topped with only crumbs that Douglas looked up at her.

"What? You expected me to stop eating and give you feedback? Impossible. You know how everyone always says you only need three bites of a dessert to be satisfied? Well, they are wrong, and have obviously never tasted anything you've made. I'm not sure I can walk out of here at this point, but if you put something else in front of me, I would eat it. I would probably die. But death by chocolate would be a wonderful way to go." Douglas smiled as he daintily wiped his mouth with a cloth napkin.

That's when he took a sip of the hot cocoa.

Icelyn watched as his eyes rolled back before he closed them completely and sighed.

"What is in this? It has to be magic!"

"That's Icelyn's specialty, but she's worried it's too basic to enter into the hot cocoa competition. She won't believe me when I say it's the best thing I've ever tasted," Holly said, crossing her arms in a huff.

Douglas stared a second longer than necessary at Holly and her crossed arms before turning to Icelyn. "She's right, you know. I can't imagine tasting anything that would beat this. It tastes like liquid magic. There's magic in it, right?"

"It's made with love, I'm sure that's what you taste," Icelyn said.

Even if there was a dash of magic in what she made, she would never admit it.

Chapter Four

Dru and Stacey dragged Colden into Mother Maude's, talking nonsense the entire way. He did everything he could to stop their progress towards the restaurant that, sadly, did not look as inviting as the chocolate shop he was being pulled away from. The one Douglas, that traitor, had just walked into. With a sigh Colden gave in and let himself be directed into the overly dark tea and coffee house.

The doors creaked as Dru pulled it open, stepping aside to let Colden and Stacey pass. The room was floor-to-ceiling wood, which should have been cozy, but instead was oppressive. He felt like the ceiling was closing in on him. Stacey stopped next to a very large table surrounded by rickety benches.

"I'm going to bring you a mug of our famous hot cocoa, everyone in town just adores it, it's won the hot cocoa contest the last five years, and maybe I'll include a baked good or two on the tray," Stacey chirped and ran off to the kitchen.

Dru sat, pulling Colden down with him. "So, is it true? Are you taking over the Snow Solstice Festival?"

"How did you hear about that already? My father just assigned me the task this morning." Colden looked at Dru, bewildered that this stranger knew about things that still felt very new to him. Did he know about his other assignment as well?

"Word travels fast in Wynterfell. Especially if there's a possibility of things changing. And you being in charge of the festival—that's a huge change. Especially if it ends with you announcing your upcoming nuptials." Dru leaned forward on the table and waited for the prince to say something.

"I have been tasked with running the festival this year," Colden said in clipped tones.

"That's fantastic! Are you planning on changing much? My family has been providing the food and hot cocoa for the event for years. We've even won the hot cocoa competition for the last five years." Dru turned to look back into the kitchen, standing as he did so.

"I would love to give it all a taste. Maybe we can set something up for another time." Colden pushed himself up: it seemed like the perfect moment to escape the dreary restaurant.

Little did he know how wrong he was, as his plan to leave was foiled when Stacey bounced back into the room carrying a tray full of treats. Dru pushed the prince back down until he was sitting on the bench, giving Colden a little squeeze before he took a seat himself.

Colden sat there, trapped. He couldn't very well get up and leave. These two were his people. However, they were only two of his people, and he wanted to walk through all of Wynterfell and discover what the majority of the town wanted for the festival, not just the ones in this room.

Dru locked eyes with Stacey and nodded. Colden had a feeling he knew what that meant, and he didn't like it. The squeal that came out of the bouncy blonde confirmed what the nod meant. Everyone in town knew he was looking for someone to be his. Stacey rushed over to his side. The tray she was carrying clattered on the table.

"Oh Prince Colden, it's true! You're announcing your spouse at the Snow Solstice Festival?"

Stacey sat so close to him that she was almost in his lap.

He gently slid away from her; that was, until he ran into Dru. The two of them had him surrounded.

Stacey scootched closer to him, pinning him between her and her twin. "Here's what I brought for you to try: a peppermint drop brownie, a pumpkin roll filled with tart cheese frosting, a cranberry-orange spice cupcake, and finally, a pomegranate gingerbread cheesecake. And to finish it all off, here's our pumpkin spice hot cocoa that won the festival competition last year."

The desserts all looked good, nicely decorated, with yummy-looking colors. There just wasn't enough chocolate on the plate in front of him. Colden's favorite desserts all included chocolate. In fact, he didn't really think it counted as a dessert unless there was chocolate involved, which was why his hand immediately sought the peppermint drop brownie.

He brought it to his lips expecting a moist chocolate bite with a crisp minty finish, like the feeling of stepping outside into the snow after sitting by a roaring fire. Instead, he almost broke a tooth. The brownie was as hard as a rock;

instead of being warm and gooey, it could be used as a weapon. He set the brownie aside, taking a sip of the hot cocoa which was bland and sour. Colden gulped it down, the only other option would have been to spit it out, which was the opposite of princely.

"So, Prince Colden, do you absolutely love it?" Stacey asked.

"That's not the word I would use?" Colden stood, only to be pushed down again.

"Scrumptious, is that a better word?" Dru leaned in, his hand on the prince's shoulder.

"If you say so."

Stacey vibrated with energy next to him. "Try the next one, it'll make your taste buds sing."

Colden took a deep breath, bracing himself for whatever came next on the plate in front of him. He grabbed the cranberry-orange spice cupcake. He took a bite—and it felt like every bit of liquid in his mouth evaporated. He coughed, causing bits of cake to come flying from his mouth. He went to grab the hot cocoa but stopped before his hand reached the cup. Dry mouth or that awful concoction, Colden didn't know which was worse.

What he did know was that he wasn't going to sit here and eat another bite. He didn't understand how this place won last year based on what he tasted today.

"If you'll excuse me, I have somewhere I need to be." Colden pushed the bench back and stood.

"But Prince Colden, you haven't tried all the tasty treats," Stacey whined. She stood there with hands on her hips and a pouty face.

"It can't be helped, duties and all that."

"At least let us put these in a box for you." Dru tried to push the prince back onto the bench. But Colden was done, he wasn't going to stay any longer.

"I'm sorry, I must be on my way. Maybe another time." Colden stepped over the bench and all but ran to the door. He had to leave the tasteless restaurant as fast as he could.

The twins had other ideas: Stacey somehow reached the door before him. "Are you going to hire us for the festival? We can make all the hot cocoa and desserts that are needed."

"We would be happy to serve you, Prince Colden . . . and everyone else at the festival," Dru said, lightly caressing Colden's shoulders.

Stacey moved in front of him and took him by the lapels. At first Colden was seriously confused, but he figured it out as she yanked him down. He moved to his right, ducking under her arm. She stumbled forward but found her balance too quickly for Colden's liking.

For a moment, he was free of her, his path out of the restaurant within reach. That was until Stacey darted in front of the door. Once again, she stood between him and his escape. His jaw clenched. This woman was on his very last nerve. He picked Stacey up and moved her out of his way. With a quick wave, he left Mother Maude's behind.

Chapter Five

Prince Colden took a deep breath the second he stepped out of the tea and coffee house. It had been suffocating in there, with the dark ceiling pressing down and the lack of fresh air. A chill went up his spine as he heard the door behind him creak. Terrified that the twins were coming out, he considered bursting into an undignified run to get away as fast as he could. He didn't take the time to look over his shoulder until he was standing by the skating pond. He stopped and stood at the railing to watch the skaters go by. Some were graceful, others could barely keep their feet under them, and then there were those who took it up a notch, turning, weaving, and brimming with joy while showing off their talents.

"They are having a lot of fun out there," a familiar voice said.

Colden looked over to see the captain of the guard standing next to him. "You abandoned me to those vultures."

Douglas threw his head back laughing. "You're right. I left you to the twins, while I tried a fabulous new place that just opened in town." Douglas held out a steaming mug. "I brought you some peppermint hot cocoa that's going to change your life."

"You think a mug of hot cocoa is going to be enough for me to forgive you? I should make you try the desserts the twins forced upon me. That's the sort of retribution you deserve. Maybe then I could find some forgiveness—maybe." The prince crossed his arms and turned away from his guard in a way reminiscent of a child pouting because his parents took away his favorite toy.

"Are you really going to turn down a delicious warm and comforting beverage over—let's call it a—misunderstanding."

"Misunderstanding, my ass. You intentionally left me alone with those harpies. They already knew about Snow Solstice and my assigned quest for a spouse. Both Dru and Stacey kept flirting with me. Plus, they served me the hardest, most awful tasting desserts I've ever had in my life. How do they stay in business? How have they won the hot cocoa competition for the last five years with bland and sour cocoa? It's incomprehensible!" Colden turned back to face Douglas with an incredulous look on his face.

"Maybe they had some help. A different baker or barista?" Douglas questioned.

"They didn't mention anyone, which seems unfair if there was someone else working there. Their attitude definitely doesn't match the reason for the season and all that," the prince said with a roll of his eyes.

Douglas held out the mug one more time. This time Colden took it. He sniffed the mug with suspicion before taking a sip. The moment the hot liquid hit his mouth, his eyes fluttered closed; the rich creamy chocolate assaulted his senses, followed by the crisp wintery taste of peppermint. He couldn't help but let out a content sigh.

"I think I'm in love," whispered Colden.

"See, I told you the cocoa would make it all worth it. Have you ever tasted anything like it?"

"This is what peppermint and chocolate taste like in my dreams, but never in real life. I have to meet the person who made this."

"It shouldn't be that hard, the business is here in town. In fact . . ."

"You don't understand, Douglas. Whoever made this drink is the *one*, the person I will marry."

The skaters closest to the prince halted their progress around the rink, straining to hear what he would say next.

"I was thinking you could hire the new chocolatier to provide cocoa for all the events. No need to go and marry them. It would be a win-win. The café would get exposure from the festival, and you would get to drink this cocoa for the entire season."

Prince Colden turned to the skaters twirling around on the ice, holding his mug with both hands. The cocoa was delicious. He took another sip, and he swore his heart fluttered. Would the maker of this cocoa understand what he was feeling, or would they think him crazy? Maybe he should take a step back and just offer them the festival contract. One of the purposes of the festival was to help local businesses, and if he did this, he would have to meet the maker of this amazing drink. It seemed like a perfect solution to at least one of the many decisions he had to make in the next couple of days. He stood and turned towards his friend.

"Okay, Douglas, let's give them a shot. They can provide hot cocoa for the first event of the festival. I believe that's the snow sculpture competition. If they can handle the first day, the booth is theirs for the rest of the festival."

Douglas whooped, drawing even more attention to him and the prince. "Of course, they'll be so excited. They've been having problems getting people into the café because of some annoying twins."

"So, I'm not the only one who's been deterred by them? And here I thought I was special."

"It appears you are quite special." Douglas gestured to the hoard of women pointing at the prince. It wasn't long before the crowd mobilized with one goal in mind: capture the prince, capture his heart. "You best run and hide; I'll distract them for as long as I can." Douglas stepped forward, laughing at Colden's plight.

"Thanks friend, nice to know you're still on my side." Colden threw the hood of his cloak over his head and made his way into a crowd that was unaware of the commotion and the fact that he was in town.

The news that he was searching for a spouse was going to make planning the festival harder. He wanted to know what would serve his kingdom best, but now he was being hunted. Maybe that was a bit dramatic, but he'd felt hunted from the moment the twins had set their eyes on him. If this was how it was going to be, he wasn't sure if he would make it to the festival, much less be able to plan the event that was needed and wanted by the people. Maybe he should make the winner of the hot cocoa contest his partner. As long as they entered, the person who made that peppermint hot cocoa, the only person he wanted by his side, would win.

The snow glistened on the tree branches as he meandered through the nearly empty park. The blue skies and the snow-covered trees were a magical sight. This was what he wanted every aspect of the festival to feel like: something magical, but also comforting. He wanted the festival to be the perfect escape into a familiar and cozy world. He could picture this park decorated with twinkling lights along the pathway leading to town. In town he could see all the festive stands with happy people selling their wares. Every stall filled with goodies, art, crafts, clothes, furniture, snacks, baked goods . . . really a little bit of anything and everything. At the end of the market, there would be a stage for different shows, and an area for his family. He wished he could participate along with everyone else, but the townsfolk would have more fun if they weren't worried about offending him. So, he would sit and watch others enjoying the entire festival, but not get to enjoy any of the events himself.

Colden had done a good job getting to a place where he was feeling extremely sorry for himself when he saw her.

She was an absolute vision of winter with hair that reminded him of light filtering through icicles; all the colors of the rainbow were present, but soft and sparkly, like the glitter of sunlight on the snow. Who was this person, and how could he be drawn to her when it felt like his heart already belonged to another?

Chapter Six

One person, that's it. The twins were successful at driving away all but the prince's guard.

Icelyn ran her hand through her hair, then shivered. She really needed to get back to her café, but it was hard to bake all morning, then sit around all day not selling a single item. She wasn't sure how much longer she could handle it. Her teeth chattered. Definitely time to head back; it was way too cold to be out without her cloak and hat, which she had left on the hooks at her café.

"Hello," someone called out in the distance. Despite living in Wynterfell the majority of her life, the only people she knew were those Holly introduced her to. Icelyn had always kept to herself in the background. It was the only way to avoid the anger of Maude and the twins. Which was why she kept on walking, ignoring the voice in the distance.

That was, until the owner of the voice was walking right beside her.

Icelyn stopped, shocked anyone was out in the glen behind her café. Earlier in the day the weather had turned bitterly cold, even for Wynterfell, causing many of the locals to stay home or hide in local shops. She was hoping one day her shop would be one people came to when the weather turned. It hadn't happened . . . yet.

"I'm sorry, I didn't realize you were talking to me. Most people don't even realize that I'm around," she babbled, taking in the handsome man beside her. He was tall, not as tall or as brawny as Douglas was, but still tall with visible strength. His blue eyes were so light they almost looked like snow, a stark contrast to his nearly black hair; and then there was the timbre of his voice . . . Let's just say, she wouldn't say no to him reading her a bedtime fairy tale any night he wanted. Just the thought of that made her shiver.

"You're cold; here, take my cloak. It's too cold to be out here without some extra layers." He looked down at her pale-blue wool dress, embroidered blue wool overdress, and her bare hands.

"I can't take your cloak; you won't have any extra layers on." Icelyn blushed. She wanted to take his cloak and envelop herself in whatever warmth he left behind.

"I can't let an enchanting lady like you shiver when I can do something that will help. What sort of man would I be if I did?"

"An average one," she muttered.

He gallantly shrugged his cloak off and swept it around her shoulders, closing it around her neck. Their eyes locked for a moment, a moment that both felt like an eternity and yet over too soon.

"Did you say something?" he asked.

"What?" She shook her head to clear her thoughts. "No, I didn't, I mean . . . If I did, it wasn't meant for anyone but me."

"Do you talk to yourself often then?"

"Of course, I almost always understand what I'm saying." Icelyn rolled her eyes. She couldn't believe she said that. Although she shouldn't really be surprised. After years living her life behind the scenes at Mother Maude's, she wasn't used to people noticing her. Especially when she was out by herself. Holly was the one who always talked to other people, dragging Icelyn along with her. Icelyn preferred to stay in the background, observing others. Every time she had ended up the center of attention, she was belittled by her stepmother and step-siblings, so she did whatever she could to avoid it. She dragged her thoughts back to the present to hear the gentleman talking. "I'm sorry, I'm afraid I wasn't actually listening."

"I should be the one who's sorry, boring you already and we just met." Laughter shined in his eyes. "I was asking for your name."

"I don't know if I should answer, my mother told me never to give my name to strangers."

"Are you playing coy with me?" the handsome man asked with suspicion.

"No, why?" Icelyn was confused.

"It's surprising to me that you don't recognize me. Colden Whittaker, at your service." He bowed with a flourish.

Shocked, Icelyn dropped into a curtsy. "I'm so sorry, Your Highness. I should have recognized you. Please forgive me."

The prince gently pulled her up from the curtsy. "There's nothing to forgive. It was just a bit of a shock to find someone in town who didn't instantly recognize me. I've felt hunted most of the day."

The two of them continued walking through the forest on the outskirts of town, Icelyn wrapped in the prince's cloak. She was struggling not to let the ends of the cloak drag in the snow, worried if she did so, she would trip on it and fall on her face. Now that she knew she was wearing the prince's cloak, she didn't want him to see her struggles, just her appreciation of the warmth surrounding her.

"Oh, that sounds awful. I would probably avoid town altogether. To be scrutinized by everyone, every second you're around. I would be exhausted."

"When you put it that way, it makes me wonder why I ever come into town. But, in all honesty, I love it here. I would come down more often if I could."

"I didn't know you came down at all," Icelyn said.

"You didn't know? Are you new to Wynterfell?"

"No, but I was never allowed out much. My stepmother had me baking in the kitchen or working in the house most of the time. I was normally left behind whenever she knew royalty was visiting; that is, unless she wanted me to bake something for your family."

"You bake? Are you going to have a booth at the Snow Solstice Festival?"

"I'm not sure. My business is struggling right now. It's nearly impossible to afford both a booth and the lease on my shop, at least not until business picks up."

"Wouldn't having your goods available at the festival mean more customers? It's supposed to help local businesses, not be hard for them to participate." Colden looked genuinely confused. He didn't understand her predicament at all.

"The stalls cost money to rent for the event. I'm not making enough at my shop to pay for a booth in the festival and keep my doors open, especially since I'll have to hire someone to work the store or at the festival. Either that, or close up my store, and I don't know if I'll sell enough to cover the cost of both."

"I had no idea." The prince stroked his chin, deep in thought. "I'm going to have to change that. Everyone who wants to participate should be able to. It's the whole point of the festival—to give the merchants another avenue to reach more customers, not worry about whether or not participating is the right choice."

"That would help out a lot of people. Right now, only the most established places participate in the Snow Solstice marketplace. Anyone who's new or struggling hopes the foot traffic from the event will keep them busy."

"I have to get back to the castle so I can put these ideas into effect in time for the festival. I'm surprised my father has never thought of any of this before." He ran his hand through his hair, causing it to become even more disheveled.

She glanced at him then down at her feet before speaking. "Not to sound impertinent, but why would your father, or your brother and sister, or anyone else in your family, think of any of these things? None of you have tried to start a business or break away from the path laid out for you. Plus, you have other concerns like maintaining the infrastructure of the town."

The prince was silent for a moment, causing her nerves to manifest as a million butterflies in her stomach.

"Can we meet again? I would love to hear more about the festival from a business perspective. Not to mention, I would love to spend more time with you. After this morning, our walk was a breath of fresh air in more ways than one."

"That would be lovely." Icelyn unbuttoned the cloak.

"No, you keep it, until next time." The prince took her hand and placed a brief kiss on the back of it, then turned and walked back into town.

Chapter Seven

The town of Wynterfell was vibrating with energy as Icelyn walked back to her café after the brief interlude with the prince. Shopkeepers were putting up decorations in their windows, carpenters were building the stalls for the marketplace, and castle servants were collecting entries for different contests. It looked like the snow sculpture contest was going to be the first event of the festival.

A gust of wind tugged at the prince's cloak. She grabbed the edges, pulling them closer around her. That's when people started to notice her. Suddenly, or so it seemed, townsfolk stopped whatever they were doing to watch her walk through town. Some gestured for their friends and neighbors to come closer, which led to a lot of pointing at her as she tried to scurry by. The peaceful walk was now anything but peaceful.

It wasn't until Stacey and Dru stepped out of their restaurant, arguing as always, that she was clued into why her very presence was causing such a raucous.

Stacey pushed her way in front of Dru. "She's wearing Prince Colden's cloak," she wailed. "It's not fair! I saw him first."

"Are you sure, Stacey? I can't see the prince acknowledging our stepsister, much less interacting with her and giving up the clothing keeping him warm," Dru drawled, pushing himself in front of Stacey.

"I would recognize that cloak anywhere," Stacey huffed, her hands on her hips.

Dru pushed his way past Stacey. "Oh my gods, you're right. How did she get it?" he asked with disgust, his voice rising to an octave she didn't believe a human could reach.

She pulled the cloak tighter around her and hiked the layers of her dress up so she could dart across the street and into her café. The bell tinkled as Icelyn opened the door. It was warm and cozy and smelled of everything deliciously sweet that was made in a kitchen. The sights and sounds pushed away the bit of unpleasantness Stacey and Dru had blessed her with. She stopped to take a deep breath before walking towards the counter where Holly was talking to someone. Their laughter filled the shop, a sound she wanted to hear every day.

"Oh, Icelyn, you're back. Douglas has returned and says he as some rather exciting news for you." Holly bounced with excitement.

"Did he tell you what it was?"

"No, so get your butt over here so I can find out what's happening." Holly skipped over to Icelyn, grabbed her hands, and pulled her the rest of the way into the café.

"Holly, give me a moment to take care of some things first, like hang up this cloak so it doesn't get ruined." She took off the cloak and hung it on one of the many cloak hooks in the room.

The bell tinkled again, alerting everyone in the room to the entrance of someone else, hopefully another customer.

Icelyn turned to see a gaggle of people come into the café. Everyone who entered paused as they stepped through the doorway and looked around, taking in the eclectic decor. Thankful for her keen attention to detail for distracting the mass of townsfolk, Icelyn had time to get behind the bakery counter.

"I know that look, I've seen it many times in my life, always after I've been spotted with the prince," Douglas said, warning Icelyn of what was coming.

"Welcome to my chocolate café," Icelyn said in an attempt to gain control of the situation. She should have stopped there, but instead she asked, "How can I help you?"

A petite woman with black curly hair with a bright red scarf holding the ringlets out of her eyes leaned on to the counter. "How do you know the prince? Do you know who he's going to marry—is he going to marry you?"

"I—um—what I meant was, can I offer you a baked good or a specialized hot cocoa?" Icelyn held up a plate of her confections.

"I guess, but what I prefer is information. But if I have to buy a treat to get the dirt, I will." The woman leaned back to look at the display of goodies. "I'll have that one." She pointed to the peppermint-mocha cupcake.

"Excellent choice. Anything to drink?"

"Do you have any seasonal tea?"

"I have a Snow Solstice blend with warm flavors like cinnamon and nutmeg balanced with some citrus notes."

"Perfect, I'll have one of those. Now, will you answer my questions?"

"I'm not sure I have any answers for you, but I'll try. First, can I get a name for the order? There's a line forming behind you." Icelyn glanced up, it was more of a crowd than a line, but she could hope.

"Tasha, I'm a reporter for the *Town Tattler*."

"Oh, so you want answers for professional reasons. I really don't want to be the center of any of this, especially since it's not much of a story," Icelyn backpedaled.

"I can leave your name out of it, not that it matters much in a town like this. But really getting in the paper can only help. This looks like a new business and one that hasn't been busy. I can help you out, just a mention in the paper will get you some patrons."

"Okay, but it's not a very interesting tale. I was in the forest behind my shop. The prince said hi to me. I was cold so he gave me his cloak, we talked, and then he left."

"That's it . . . ? I'm sure there is more." Tasha leaned in.

"No, we chatted; he only talked about the Snow Solstice Festival. He's trying to make the marketplace more accessible to local shop owners."

"At least that's something." Tasha took a bite of the cupcake. Her eyes went wide, she stopped moving completely, then her eyes fluttered shut and she moaned, "Oh my gods, so good."

Icelyn smiled. She loved watching a person's first taste of her baking; it was the truest form of praise because it was unfiltered.

"You made this?" Tasha asked.

"Of course, I made everything here." Icelyn's smile was so wide it lit up her entire face.

"Icelyn, we need more of . . . everything!" Holly screeched.

Icelyn looked at the full café, the empty cases, and her panicked friend. Holly had handled the crowd like a professional until there was nothing left to serve.

"I'm sorry, but I'm going to have to close shop today, but I will be open tomorrow with enough goodies for everyone."

A groan went through the crowd as Douglas and Holly escorted everyone out. Icelyn hoped everyone would come back tomorrow, or at least *some* of the people who had followed her in would come back tomorrow. She also hoped she had enough ingredients to bake for actual customers.

"Whew, what happened to bring all those people in here?" Holly asked.

"I met the prince, and he loaned me his cloak. People noticed."

"People tend to do that around here," Douglas said with a laugh.

"At least it was good for business. Even if they were just here for gossip, they all bought something—that is, until we ran out." Holly plopped into one of the comfy chairs. "I'm used to nothing happening here, and that was a nice, but exhausting, change."

"It was fantastic, I can't believe I sold out. Now Douglas, what is this news you have for us." Icelyn leaned against Holly's chair.

"I brought Colden a mug of your cocoa: peppermint and chocolate happens to be his favorite. I suggested that you could provide hot cocoa for the events during the festival."

"And . . ." Holly leaned forward.

"He's not an ignorant man. He said yes, of course. And then people started to notice him, so he took off to hide in the forest."

"Which is when he met me. Did you tell him about me at all?"

"No, just that the café I went to was struggling because of the twins. And he wanted to help, especially since they had trapped him and fed him their baked wares."

"Oh no, they can't bake anything worth eating. I spent the last five years in that kitchen. Without me there, it can't be good."

"So, you're the reason they've won the hot cocoa competition the last five years, and you're worried you wouldn't win on your own? Icelyn, it's practically in the bag, you have to enter," Douglas said.

"That's what I've been telling her for ages now." Holly looked at Icelyn pointedly, then a smile broke out. "This is going to be good; the twins are finally going to get what they deserve."

Chapter Eight

"Douglas, I'm at a loss for words; my heart and my head are confused." The sound of the prince's muffled voice emanated from the body lying face down on the grand four-poster bed.

"What has befallen you this time, my lord?" Douglas asked, unable to hide the tinge of sarcasm laced through his words.

Pushing himself up, Colden glared at his friend. "You don't have to be flippant about it. I could be in real trouble here. I think I'm in love with two different women."

"Is that so? If it's true, that could cause a problem. But you have time to figure it out. The festival hasn't even started. You can learn more about both of them over the next couple of weeks."

The look on Douglas's face as he spoke baffled Colden. It looked like Douglas was holding back laughter, but what could Douglas know that he did not?

"I don't even know who made the hot cocoa. How am I going to get to know the person better?" He sighed. The feelings that the hot cocoa provoked seemed so real.

As unlikely as it seemed, one sip and it was like he knew everything about the person who made it. He could sense her kindness, how she loved what she did, and her determination to find success all in that one sip of cocoa. Those were all the qualities he was looking for in a partner. Now that he knew she was out there, he needed to figure out a way to find her and meet her.

The squeal of his door opening caused him to turn towards it. There stood his brother Oliver, Ollie for short, panting like he had just run a foot race.

"What is it, Ollie?" Colden asked, staring at the spitting image of himself as his younger brother fought to catch his breath. "Breathe in through your nose."

"He's in a mood. I can't tell if it's a good one," Ollie panted.

"What does he want now?"

"Something about you meeting someone today. He wants to know more."

What could Colden even say about her? And if his dad learned about the hot cocoa maker, and the feelings a sip of hot cocoa inspired, the king would lose his mind.

Loud banging on the door interrupted Colden's reverie. He sighed: there was only one person who knocked with such insistence.

The king didn't wait to be let in. As he burst through, the door swung open and hit the castle wall with a bang.

Colden sighed. "What do you want, Father?" He glanced over at Ollie, mouthing the words *Thank you.*

"I heard you went into town today. Moreover, you were seen with a young lady. Does this mean you are taking my task seriously?" The king was the worst gossip in the kingdom, which made sense if one thought about the gathering-information part, but sometimes he blathered more than a group of women in a knitting circle.

"When was the last time I didn't take you seriously, Father?"

"Do you really want me to answer that?" The king raised his brow and crossed his arms.

"Probably not. I don't know if it's that I am taking your ultimatum seriously as much as it is happenstance, but I did meet some interesting people. The woman in the forest was a delight to talk to and gave me some ideas about the marketplace for the festival. She pointed out that as a struggling shopkeeper she couldn't afford a booth and hoped the foot traffic from the festival was enough to help her brick-and-mortar business. But if the goal of the marketplace is to help these small shop owners, we need to make it more accessible to everyone. Which might include finding help for those who can't afford extra employees."

The king's eyes widened. "Those are excellent points. I'm surprised you are taking the festival so seriously. Last we spoke you seemed to think it was a frivolous endeavor."

"I know, but I was put right by a dear friend." Colden looked over at Douglas. "He reminded me that the festival brought the last bit of business before the winter storms came and everyone went on lockdown."

"Ah yes, an important reminder. It's easy to forget that, living like we do in the castle on the hill. It's good to go into town and see what townsfolk want and need."

"There's a lot of excitement surrounding the festival. The first event is going to be the snow sculpture competition. I hired someone to provide hot cocoa for the event. You should have tasted the hot cocoa. It was magic." Colden closed his eyes. Just the thought of the warm concoction brought a smile to his lips.

"Are you going with Mother Maude's? We've used them for the last five years. They are a bit demanding, but I've always enjoyed their product."

"Well, Father, I decided to go with someone else. I did stop by and try some of their *things*, and I can't in good conscience hire them. It was not up to our standards this year, to put it nicely."

"That's a shame. But it will be nice to have some new flavors this year. I'm happy you are committed to the event and hopefully finding a partner. I'm not getting any younger, and I want you to have someone by your side when you take over. This isn't a job to do alone. It's been so much harder to do since your mother's death." The king blinked the tears from his eyes. It had been six years since the death of the queen, but her absence was felt in the castle every single day.

"I know, Father. You're just trying to look out for me, but this is not something that I want to rush into."

"I understand." He grabbed the door. "It makes me happy to know you are trying." He glanced over at Oliver. "You're next—don't think you've escaped my involvement. Then your sister, once it's safe for her to come home." The king clapped his arm around Oliver and shut the door behind the two of them.

Colden listened to his father's footsteps as he walked down the hallway. When there was silence, he turned to Douglas. "I have to find out who made the hot cocoa. They must enter the hot cocoa contest, and if I haven't found them before then, I will marry whoever wins."

Chapter Nine

"I can't thank you enough, Holly. I'm going to need so much help getting everything baked today, especially if we have a crowd like yesterday. As much as I hate the fact that they were all here for gossip and not my baked goods, I'm glad they were in here. Hopefully, they come back for the food." Icelyn unlocked the door to the café.

Holly's teeth chattered as she stood there in the morning fog. "Just remember that I'm here for you. In the cold. While it's still dark outside. Why do you get up before the sun? Is it some sort of masochistic punishment?"

Icelyn pushed the door open and stepped aside, gesturing for Holly to go ahead. "It's not punishment; there's nothing like waking up and starting the morning surrounded by the smell of baked goods and roasting coffee."

"If you say so, but now that you mention it, I wouldn't say no to something made with those roasted coffee beans." She rubbed her eyes.

"How about a spicy mocha? I was thinking about serving them at the snow sculpture competition. You can be my official tester."

"You know I can't say no to an offer like that; it's my main purpose in life to try everything you make."

Icelyn laughed as she went around the café turning on each of the lights. She heard Ember let out a puff to start the fire, or that's what she thought was happening, which was why she didn't turn around and continued her normal morning routine. Ember let out another puff, followed by a long whine.

"Oh my gods. Icelyn, your kitchen . . . your supplies . . . It's a disaster."

Icelyn stopped what she was doing and slowly turned to see Holly standing there, frozen in one spot, mouth agape, staring at the kitchen. Icelyn followed her gaze.

"What in the . . ." Icelyn couldn't believe her eyes. It was a mess. Chocolate was all over the stove. Flour and cocoa and sugar covered every surface: the floor, the counters, the drawer fronts, even the knobs were coated in baking ingredients. She dropped to the floor, tears streaming down her face. She was ruined. There was no way she would be able to recover from the damage. If she didn't open today, all the momentum from yesterday would disappear. Her café would be yesterday's news, and everyone would forget about her.

"Oh Icelyn, sweetie, we'll fix it. I'm sure we can figure something out."

"How? I can't make anything if I don't have ingredients. And I can't get ingredients at this hour. On top of that, I can't afford to buy everything again. There's only so much money . . ." Icelyn drifted off; her eyes darted to the front desk. "My cash box . . . did they get that too?"

She pushed herself up off the floor, stumbling as she ran to the front. It was there, the box her mother had given her. It was one of the few things she had from her mother; she used it to keep her most valuable and cherished items in, and she had started to use it as her cash box when she opened the café because it was nice to have something from her mother with her every day. Icelyn cried in relief that the box was still there. She opened the box, and everything was still in it: her profits from yesterday, the smaller box of sentimental trinkets she kept around for luck, and her family's recipe book.

"At least you can purchase more supplies. Even if you open late, it will help keep you in business. Do you want me to contact the sheriff?" Holly asked.

"No, I'm pretty sure I know who did this, and nothing bad ever happens to them. Let's clean up the store, and I'll see what I can do about buying more ingredients." Icelyn sighed; it was going to be a long, expensive day.

There was a tap on the door. Icelyn slumped, laying her head down on the table. "What now?"

"Don't worry, I'll send whoever it is away. Then I'll start cleaning up the back for you." Holly patted Icelyn's back before she answered the door.

Icelyn didn't know what she would do if she didn't have Holly. It was nice to have someone around who always had her back. She looked up to watch as Holly sent away whoever was at the door this early in the morning.

"Douglas!" Holly squealed. "I'm so glad you're here. We are desperate for some help." She grabbed the burly man's hand and dragged him to the kitchen.

"Holly, you don't need to involve Douglas. It's really not something he should be concerned with."

"Don't be ridiculous, Icelyn. I'm here to help any way that I can," Douglas said. "That's not technically true, I'm here for more sweets, but I'll do whatever I need to do to get more of what you baked." Douglas turned to the kitchen. "Oh my gods, what happened here? Did you call the sheriff?"

"No, I don't want to start anything. I just want to fix what happened." Icelyn pulled back her hair, preparing to get to work.

"You should report this. No one should go through this and not try to have the culprit caught." Douglas ran his hand through his hair.

"Nothing ever happens to the people that I think did this. They are slippery and have always covered their tracks. I've spent years letting them make my life miserable, and I'm not going to do it anymore." Icelyn grabbed a broom; she was ready to get down to business.

"She's talking about the twins. After her mother left, her father married Maude. He thought he was doing the right thing, but Dru and Stacey were terrible to her. Every time her father left town for work, Maude was just as bad as the twins, treating her like a servant instead of family." Holly filled Douglas in on the history Icelyn would rather ignore.

Douglas turned Icelyn around. "Give me a list of everything you need to run the shop today. I'll go shopping while you clean."

Icelyn shook her head. "I can't have you do that, I'm sure you're busy. Don't you have things to take care of for the prince? No, I'll clean and then shop. I'll just have to close today and re-open tomorrow."

"You can't close, you need to open as if nothing happened. It will drive the twins batty." Holly looked at Icelyn with mischievous glee.

"What are you plotting?"

"Nothing more than what you were planning on doing, anyway: We ignore this happened. Go about business as usual. They'll die if you don't act like you are devastated."

"It's not much of a revenge, but it is something." She leaned on the broom as she contemplated Holly's plan.

"I would really like to help; I was here to negotiate the details of the festival cocoa deal, anyway. The prince doesn't expect me back for a while," Douglas said.

It was like Douglas was her fairy godmother, swooping in to fix her problems. She couldn't help but giggle at the image that formed in her head. The burly captain of the guard, with delicate wings and a fairy wand, flittering around, making her wishes come true. She quickly covered her mouth to stifle her giggle.

Icelyn looked from Holly to Douglas, both looking at her expectantly.

She threw her hands up in the air. "Fine, I'll make a list, and you can go to the market for me. Holly and I will clean. And hopefully, I'll be able to get something done in time to open at a decent hour."

Chapter Ten

"Where have you been, Douglas?" Colden asked as he threw his hands up in frustration. "Opening day of the Snow Solstice Festival is only two days away, and there's so much more to do."

"Exactly, I was taking care of one of the tasks you set out for me. I was with the new café owner. I went there to nail down the terms for them to supply the hot cocoa for all the festival events." Douglas sat in one of the oversized chairs in the prince's quarters.

The prince paced. "What took you so long? It should have been a simple task, not something that took all day. I should have gone; I missed a chance to discover who made the magical hot cocoa."

"I'm sorry, Your Highness," Douglas said with a sarcastic bow of his head. "There was some trouble at the café. It took all day to make everything right." He stood.

Colden stopped pacing. "Trouble? What kind of trouble?"

Douglas poured Icelyn's newest hot cocoa recipe into two of the prince's new hand-warmer mugs he purchased from Icelyn's café. He handed one mug to the prince, taking the other back to his seat.

"Their entire stock of ingredients was destroyed. Bakers bake all morning long to get ready for the day. Instead of baking, they had to clean, and I offered to go to the market for them so they would be able to open today," Douglas explained.

"Do you know who did this to them?" Colden sat, leaning forward as he did so. He held his hot cocoa in his hands but did not drink. There was a determined glint in his eyes.

"The owner and her best friend think it was the twins. Apparently, there's a lifelong animosity there." Douglas took a sip of the spicy mocha Icelyn had sent home with him.

Colden leaned back in his chair, still holding his mug as he took in the information. The twins, they were quite a pair, but to ransack someone else's business was beyond the pale.

"I should go talk to them. Let them know what's in their future if they continue. This kingdom does not put up with that type of behavior."

"I don't think that's a good idea. The proprietor doesn't want to draw that type of attention to her café, so she asked us to ignore it. Let the twins think it didn't have an effect on her." Douglas sat back in the chair, relaxed, hot drink in hand.

Colden sat there deep in thought, his hands wrapped around his mug, still filled with the hot drink because he had yet to take a sip. What was going on in town that his citizens were out harming others? He felt like his hands were tied, but he wanted to do something now to stop what was happening and prevent it from happening again in the future.

He raised the mug to his lips but lowered it before taking a sip. It was two days until the opening of the festival. He needed to stay focused on the plans and avoid any town shenanigans.

"My gods, man, are you ever going to take a sip of the drink I poured for you?" Douglas interrupted Colden's thoughts.

"What?" He looked down at the mug in his hands. "Oh yes, of course." Colden took a sip of the chocolate drink. It was rich with chocolate, enhanced by a hint of coffee, but what made it special was the hint of cinnamon and cayenne. It was something that was both comfortable, yet at the same time it was different enough to push boundaries. It reminded him of the first time you hugged a person you had feelings for. The hug was exciting because there's something more coming.

Just like the last cup of cocoa, this one tasted like love.

Colden looked around at everything going on in the town square. The place vibrated with energy as he oversaw the setup for the festival. Blue and silver decorations hung across the sidewalks and roads. There were lights hanging from the trees, around the light post, practically everywhere. The noise of building the booths for the shopkeepers was the song of the town. The hammers provided the rhythm, while the saws and other tools sang the melody. Shouts of the townsfolk putting up lights and signs filled the air. As annoyed as he was that this ended up in his lap, seeing it all go together put a smile on his frozen face.

Tomorrow was the snow sculpture competition. The area was ready with fresh snow from a late-night storm. The banners were hung, and the hot cocoa booth was set up, waiting for the proprietor to arrive.

Colden stood nearby. He planned to meet this person today. However, he saw a purple dragon flying around on the end of a leash held by the woman he met in the forest. He looked back at the hot cocoa booth and then towards Icelyn.

"Douglas, I'll be right back, there's someone I need to go talk to." Colden looked back long enough to see Douglas nod.

He made his way through the crowd until he was standing in front of the pretty young woman with multicolored hair that sparkled in the winter light like a layer of fresh snow.

"Hello, I didn't expect to see you again so soon." Colden fell into step beside Icelyn.

"Oh, Your Highness . . ." Icelyn curtsied as she walked, tripping over her own feet as she did so.

Colden grabbed her arm. "Colden is fine, and there's no need for you to curtsy."

"Okay . . . This is only my second time talking to a prince, and I'm really not sure what to do." Icelyn took a step back, out of the hands of the prince.

"There's nothing to do. I don't need any special treatment, especially from you." He smiled the lopsided smile he was known for. "Let's go for a walk."

Icelyn took his arm with a small smile before she looked away. "What are you doing in town today, Your . . . I mean . . . Colden?"

"Tomorrow is the first day of the Snow Solstice Festival. It starts with the snow sculpture competition, and I just wanted to make sure everything would be ready for tomorrow."

"Everyone is so busy; do you think it's all going to get done in time?"

Colden looked at the chaos around them. In all honesty, the town didn't look anywhere near to being ready, but he could envision it coming together. In every event there was that moment where things looked impossible. It was always followed by everything coming together just the way it needed to.

"It always has in the past. I won't let my first year running the event be the one time everything doesn't get done on time. I should probably get back to work. I hope I'll see you at the competition tomorrow." He pressed a light kiss on the back of Icelyn's gloved hand before walking away.

Chapter Eleven

"I can't believe the festival starts today! How are we on supplies? Do you think I have enough to make it through the day?" Icelyn chewed on her thumbnail as she looked at the cart she and Holly had loaded.

Her plan for the festival was to have two blends of hot cocoa each day: one, a standard hot cocoa with the richness and creaminess everyone expects when they take a sip of cocoa; the other, a special blend. Today's was the spicy mocha she had tested yesterday.

In the cart there were stacks of boxed baked goods she had been putting together since three in the morning, next to those were bags of different types of chocolate, glass bottles of her signature oat milk, and jars of cinnamon and cayenne. It looked like everything was packed and ready to go.

"Oh my gods, I almost forgot the coffee beans. That would have been a disaster." Icelyn shook her head.

Holly grabbed Icelyn's shoulders, forcing her to stop and make eye contact. "It's all going to be fine; you've practically packed up your entire shop. I think you have everything you need. If you don't, I can come back and get it for you. Just take a deep breath and enjoy the moment."

Icelyn sighed, swatting away Holly's hands. "It's such a huge opportunity. I can't afford to mess this up."

She ran back into the store as Holly called after her. "You won't mess anything up. I don't think you know how, especially when it comes to your magical concoctions."

The door to her shop closed behind her, muffling Holly's pep talk. Icelyn looked from shelf to shelf for the roasted coffee beans, feeling her panic levels rise as she turned up empty-handed after looking in so many different areas.

"Now where did I leave those coffee beans? It's not like me to not put them back in their spot." Icelyn shrugged the tension out of her shoulders. She knew she couldn't put her hands on them because she was putting too much pressure on herself. But she couldn't stop: it was imperative this event was a success. There was no way she would waste such a wonderful opportunity.

She sighed. Of course, it would be a waste if she couldn't find her ingredients.

She took a step towards the door, giving up, her mind spinning with new recipe ideas, worried because she wouldn't have time for someone to taste whatever she decided on first. Then Ember appeared like a puff of smoke with the jar of coffee beans in her mouth, gently nudging Icelyn's hands to grab it.

"Oh my gods, Ember, you're a life saver." She swooped up the tiny dragon into a great big hug before darting to the door. "Thank you again, sweetie. If you think you can stay out of trouble, you can spend your day at the booth with me. But you have to be on your best behavior. No shenanigans." Before leaving the café, she held her pet dragon's face in her hand, making sure eye contact was made.

Ember jumped from one foot to another, flapping her wings, shaking her head yes with enthusiasm.

The door jangled as Holly poked her head in. "Now get a move on! You have hot cocoa to get into the hands of every person in Wynterfell."

Icelyn and Holly pushed the cart through the still sleepy town. The festivities were starting today, but for now the townsfolk stayed bundled up in bed, warm and cozy, at least until the sun finally rose. It was important for Icelyn to be set up before then, ready to serve her first customer as soon as the festivities started.

They arrived at the booth and unpacked everything. Ember flew to the countertop, supervising the movements of Holly and Icelyn as they organized the space. Finally, Icelyn gestured to Ember, requesting her to hop over and light the fire. Icelyn needed to get her chocolate melting so it produced that rich velvety drink everyone was expecting. In moments, her pots and pans steaming and simmering, Icelyn moved seamlessly between stirring one pot, spicing another, and adjusting the fire on another—a dance so familiar to her, in that moment, she felt like she could do it in her sleep. The comfort of what she did every day relaxed her, all the nerves she was feeling before left her body, replaced by pure joy. She hummed as she poured the first mug. The smell of chocolate and cinnamon wafted towards her as she inhaled the rich flavor, sipped the cocoa, and sighed blissfully, content with what she had made. Setting the mug down, she went back to the stove, adding a pinch of this, a dash of that, and just a bit of the happiness she felt sprinkled in with the other ingredients.

"Icelyn, this looks amazing, and smells even better. I want to try one, maybe two, of everything." Holly clapped her hands. "What do you think of the menu?" Holly held up a chalkboard. She had three things listed: traditional cocoa, dragon's breath mocha, and assorted baked goods. Next to each she had drawn a picture of the item. The sign was adorable, absolutely perfect for the event.

"It's so good, Holly! You're such a talented artist."

"This, it's nothing. Now you go walk around for a bit. You deserve a break before the crowds rush in."

"I don't know, I think I should really stay here."

Holly pushed Icelyn out of the stall. "Look, there's Douglas, I'm sure he can help while you take a small break. You've been at this for hours."

"Okay, okay, I'll go. But I won't be gone long." Icelyn left her booth and made her way through the quiet town. At least it was quiet until a bunch of screaming girls accosted Prince Colden.

Icelyn laughed. It would drive her bonkers to be followed around like he was. Ever since the king said his son would be announcing his spouse by the end of the festival, the single people in this town had lost their minds. Every time the prince came to town, he was surrounded by townsfolk trying to win his favor, making it almost impossible for him to finish the festival preparations. She watched for a minute as more women and men swarmed around him.

"Prince Colden! I have a question for you," Icelyn hollered, waving at the prince as the crowd around him turned towards her.

Colden's eyes widened at first, then recognition crossed his face, and a huge smile broke out. He muttered his apologies as he made his way through his adoring fans.

"He's going to her again. What is it about her?" Stacey stomped her foot.

"I don't know, but we need to do something about it," Dru responded, crossing his arms.

Icelyn looked over at the twins before Prince Colden demanded all her attention. He grabbed her hand and dragged her with him as he ran away from the crowd. He stopped when they arrived at the town's gazebo. The snowflakes hanging from the ceiling slowly spun as the breeze picked up. Everything in town looked extra wintery for the festival.

"Thank you, I thought I was never going to extricate myself from that group. You saved me."

"I did no such thing." Icelyn laughed.

"No really, it was a near-death situation. You are my hero." He took her hand and raised it to her lips.

She shivered as a tingling feeling climbed her spine. "Fine, I'm a hero. But I won't always be around to save you. Especially if you are planning on coming down for all the events of the festival."

"I know, and it's not going to get any better now that word is out. Now I'm hunted." He looked over his shoulder, panic in his eyes.

Icelyn threw her head back, laughing. "I wish I could help keep the hunters at bay."

Colden sat on the gazebo bench. "Actually, maybe there is something you can do to help."

Icelyn stared at the prince, eyes wide. "How can I help you? I think the only thing you could do to stop the town from following you around is to announce you are dating someone."

"That's exactly what we could do. We can pretend to be together. At least until the hot cocoa competition. People already have their suspicions just because we've been seen spending time together." Colden looked eager, like a puppy asking for a special treat.

"I don't know, it's dishonest," Icelyn hedged.

"We don't have to actually say anything, the papers will pick up on the story that's implied. Being seen with me should bring business to your shop. You did mention it was struggling the first time we spoke. This could be an opportunity for both of us." Colden grabbed her hands. His eyes pleaded for her to say yes.

She removed her hands from his and looked off into the distance. "I'm not sure, it could be good, but it feels wrong." She didn't like tricking everyone, but no one really knew her even though she had lived here her entire life. And it would give the prince the ability to really meet people, maybe even his soulmate, without being stalked by everyone in town. Maybe it wasn't such a bad idea after all; at least the two of them enjoyed each other's company. She turned to Colden. "You know what, I'll do it." She looked into his eyes with a wobbly smile on her face.

Colden whooped as he stood. He picked her up and swung her around. When he set her down, Icelyn looked around to see every eye in town on them, including her lovely step-siblings, Dru and Stacey.

Chapter Twelve

Colden was in a world of his own as he walked back to the contest site, Icelyn tucked into his side, his arm draped across her shoulders. He was oblivious to the glares focused on them by many a young person. He was unaware of the whisperings from one person to the next, all asking who the person at the prince's side was. And he failed to see how everyone in town moved out of his way as they walked through town. Most likely because he was raised to believe it was his due as prince.

He felt Icelyn's step slow, like she was hesitant to be seen with him by so many people. She then moved away from him, ever so slightly, which broke through the happy haze and let reality slowly take its place. Colden noticed the glares and whisperings for the first time.

He lowered his head to whisper in Icelyn's ear. "Are you okay?"

He felt, rather than saw, her head shake. "I'm not used to so much attention. I've lived here my entire life, and most of the people staring at me now have never acknowledged my existence before. And now, everyone seems so hostile. I was ready for more attention, or so I thought, but I was not ready for the hostility. I normally only feel that from my step-siblings." She shrugged, as if that small motion would make everything go away.

Colden looked at her with concern in his eyes. "Are you sure you want to do this? It's not too late to back out."

He waited for her to respond, afraid to take a breath until he heard her response. He didn't know her well, but knew he enjoyed spending time with her. He didn't want Icelyn to change her mind.

He continued to watch her as she looked away. "I want to do this. I just wasn't ready for everyone to be staring at me with such intensity." She turned back to him and took his hands. "Thank you, thank you for everything." She went up on her toes and kissed him on the cheek, then left, disappearing into the crowd before he could stop her.

Colden stood there floundering. Should he go after her? But, how? He didn't know where she was going, and he didn't see her anywhere among the townsfolk. He sighed. Might as well get back to the snow sculpture contest. It must be about time for the judging to commence.

He made his way through the busy streets of his kingdom, nodding at his people as they passed. The town was something to be proud of, especially with all the shimmering winter decorations up. He made his way to the snow sculpture field, which was surrounded by a red fence to designate the contest area. The field was full of different sculptures, some large, others small, all unique in their own way.

He needed his clipboard with the score sheets to start the judging, something that Douglas should have with him. He searched for his friend and guard, finally catching sight of the large man over by the hot cocoa stand, flirting with a sprite-like redhead. The two of them looked good together.

Colden made his way to the hot cocoa booth, taking note of some sculptures that stood out. There was an adorable dragon family made of snow that defied gravity, or so it seemed.

Something about how the younger dragons were sculpted to fly around the older dragon's head looked real. Then there was the sculpture Dru and Stacey were working on, a life-size version of himself. Colden rolled his eyes: those two always took things too far. There was what a reasonable person would do, and then there were the twins.

"I think I need to try today's special hot cocoa," Colden said as he leaned onto the booth. Out of the corner of his eye, he thought he saw a head of shimmery hair pop up and instantly disappear.

"Of course, Prince Colden, I will get you one right now," Holly said, distracting him from what he thought he saw.

Colden shook his head; he must have imagined it. "Are you the owner of this shop?" he asked, turning his attention to Holly completely.

"Oh my, no. My best friend is the magic behind the hot cocoa. I'm helping her out so she can take breaks and also keep her café open." Holly smiled as she handed him a mug. "I think you'll love the special she came up with today. It has a little kick to it."

Colden took a sip. The richness of the chocolate rolled around on his tongue, followed by the warmth of cinnamon and the spicy heat from the cayenne. It was the same as the drink Douglas brought him the day before, but today it was even more magical. The flavors were both mesmerizing and shocking. The melding of them insisted that he take one sip after another, each taste more nuanced than the last. What magic was this?

"It's time to start the judging," Douglas said, interrupting Colden's enjoyment of this new flavor of hot cocoa.

"I would rather wait for the maker of this cocoa to come back. It's absolute magic." Colden looked towards the booth; longing filled his eyes.

"However, duty calls." Douglas grabbed the score sheets and clipboards.

"I'm going, I'm going. Quit trying to herd me towards the competition. I'm not going to let wanting to meet someone stop me from performing my duties as prince." Colden huffed.

"I'm sorry, Your Highness." Douglas's flippant tone was sure to earn a rebuke from the prince. "You seemed a tad distracted by your love of hot cocoa."

"Or the person who made it," Colden whispered.

The snow sculpture field loomed ahead. Judging was not one of Colden's favorite princely duties, especially when it was as subjective as an art competition.

He looked at each of the sculptures, impressed with the dedication and skill the competitors had put into their designs. There was a life-size yeti where the fur looked like it would be soft if he touched it, but it was made of snow. A beautiful mermaid sunning herself on a rock was another piece that drew his attention. The rest of the entries were a variety of sprites, wood nymphs, and an assortment of local animals. Everything looked fantastic, even the sculpture of him was well done, although he hated to admit it because the twins wore on his last nerve whenever he had to interact with them. The cloak was a nice touch, though. He almost always wore—

Wait was that his cloak? The one he had lent out to the woman in the forest?

A cracking sound distracted him from the sculptures. He glanced up to see snow fall from a tree branch. His eyes followed the path of the falling snow to find Dru covered in it, trying to brush it off without much success.

Dru glared up at the tree as if that would make it feel bad for dumping the snow. It didn't; in fact, if Colden believed trees had feelings, Dru might have angered the tree even more. The next thing that happened was the branch, now empty of snow, fell onto Dru and Stacey's sculpture.

"Oh nooooo!" Stacey screamed, staring at the destroyed sculpture. "It's ruined. We were going to win for sure."

"The prince wouldn't disqualify us because we were sabotaged," Dru said, looking directly at Colden.

Maude walked over to her children, hugging Stacey. "You're right, Dru, I can't see our dearly beloved prince disqualifying you because of something out of your control."

The prince listened to the conversation, waiting for it to end before heading over to talk to the twins. He was about to tell Dru and Stacey that he would still consider their entry despite the fact it was now a mound of snow when Stacey's screams interrupted him.

"It's all her fault!" Stacey exclaimed, pointing to Icelyn. "She always ruins everything."

"It's true." Maude shook her head and *tsked.* "She's always trying to hurt my two babies. She even quit working at the café a few months ago. She tried to take our customers away from us. Thankfully, her despicable plan failed."

"It must have been the cloak! She gave it to us, and look what happened." Dru pointed to the pile of snow that was once their sculpture.

Colden stopped in his tracks. He looked over to where Stacey was pointing. He knew Icelyn; the woman he saw standing there was not the type of person who would harm others. It did surprise him that she would give away his cloak, though. Maybe the twins had mentioned what they were planning and she thought it would be a nice touch.

"What are you going to do about this horrible act, Prince Colden?" Maude prodded.

"I think I'll continue judging the competition and announce the winner once I'm done," Colden said, his tone clipped. "What I'm not going to do is blame someone for something caused by nature. Snow falls off branches and branches break. Especially this time of year."

"I'm sure she used her magic to do it. Don't you know who her mother is?" Maude continued, despite Stacey and Dru's attempts to keep their mother quiet.

"I'm sure who her mother is has nothing to do with the branch falling." Colden turned to the rest of the crowd. "Now, let's go to the stage so I can announce the winners."

The sculptors followed Colden to the stage. There he stood before everyone that entered, all of them waiting to find out if they had won.

"In third place, we have the yeti."

The crowd applauded as the sculptor took stage and accepted their prize. Colden repeated the process for the second-place winner, the gorgeous mermaid sculpture.

"And finally, the winner is *Dragons at Play*. The movement and magic in this sculpture is phenomenal. I've never seen anything like it," Colden said.

"What!" Dru and Stacey exclaimed. "How did we not win!"

Chapter Thirteen

Icelyn looked around at the disaster that was her hot cocoa stand. She had been afraid that the prince would take away her contract after Maude's accusations. Instead, she was swarmed by townsfolk for the rest of the day. Now she stood, exhausted, surrounded by a mess that needed cleaning, and with no menu or ingredients for tomorrow, she was in a bit of a bind.

"Holly, is there any cocoa left in the shop? I feel like I sent you back every hour to get more. We were so much busier than I expected." Icelyn re-tied her apron around her waist and grabbed a towel. She couldn't leave until this place was spotless.

"Nowhere near enough for tomorrow if it's as busy as it was today. I think we need more of everything." Holly sat on the counter. "Are you really going to clean now? I'm so tired."

"Go ahead and go on home. I'll finish up here, and hopefully make it to the market before it closes tonight." She piled the empty mugs into the sink.

"Don't worry about the market, Douglas talked to them earlier and asked them to stay open until you could stop by tonight. But if you want to divide and conquer, make a list, and I'll go to the store while you clean up. It's the only way you're going to get any sleep. I know you're going to be up before dawn, baking for tomorrow."

"That would help me out so much, Holly. Now to decide on the flavors for tomorrow." Icelyn tapped her quill pen on her teeth while she thought about all the different possibilities. She had narrowed it down between a gingerbread hot cocoa made with all the warming spices of fall, but wondered if that was too similar to the one she made today. Or she could make a toasted s'mores hot cocoa with marshmallows and graham crackers. Something quite the opposite from today's menu. Icelyn scribbled ingredients down for both recipes at a furious pace. "Here, Holly, this is everything I need for tomorrow."

Holly snatched the list. "Perfect, don't forget you entered Ember in the mushing event tomorrow.

You might want to find someone else to help with the booth."

"But who? You're the only person that I trust."

"Find someone and pay them. If you have another day like today, it will be worth it. Just make sure they aren't friends with Dru and Stacey."

"I'll see what I can do, Holly. Now get to the market. I don't want to make someone stay there all night."

"I'm going, I'm going." Holly jumped off the counter and skipped off, leaving Icelyn there alone.

Icelyn got to work cleaning up everything from the day. There were so many mugs to clean; all day long, mug after mug needed cleaning. Ember popped her little dragon head out from under the counter and mewed.

"I know, Ember, it's past your bedtime, and you need all the sleep you can get for the race tomorrow." She patted the little dragon's head before going back to work.

She danced through the cleaning of the tiny kitchen, making the work go so much faster than if she thought of it as drudgery. Which meant it felt like mere minutes had passed when she put away the last mug with a small smile.

"Come on, Ember. With any luck, Holly's already finished shopping, and we can be off to bed soon. What do you think of Holly racing you tomorrow?"

Ember flapped her wings, puffing a few times in excitement.

"I take it you don't mind the idea. Just remember to be on your best behavior."

"Icelyn Frost, just the woman I wanted to talk to," Tasha called out.

Hearing her name stopped Icelyn mid-step. She turned slowly. Tasha was so nice to her the last time they talked, but speaking to anyone who might print her life story in the paper made her nervous.

"Hi, Tasha. How can I help you tonight?" Icelyn asked with a sigh. She really wanted to be home, a fire going, curled up under a blanket, getting some sleep.

"I saw you with the prince again today." Tasha pulled out a notebook and pencil.

"Yes, we did spend some time together today," Icelyn hedged. She didn't know what to say. They had come to an agreement today to help each other out, but should she be telling someone at the paper? Colden hadn't really laid out any expectations for her, and now she didn't know how to navigate the situation.

"Can you give any more information than that? Is there anything between the two of you? Are sparks flying? Is it just friends? What's going on?" Tasha prodded.

"Um . . . I'm not sure what to say. I do enjoy his company." Icelyn looked away. Colden said they wouldn't have to lie, the papers would just pick up on their implied behavior, and he never mentioned what to do when confronted with the press.

"That's something, I guess." Tasha blew her curls out of her eyes. "It's not enough for an article, but maybe I can write up a teaser."

Icelyn looked down at her hands. She didn't want to say more, but she liked Tasha, and she felt like she was letting her down. "Tasha, I'm not ready to say anything, yet. But when I am, I'll come to you first. I promise. Now, I have to go, I need to find someone to help me out at the hot cocoa booth tomorrow. Holly's entered the race with Ember, and if the booth's busy like today, there's no way I'll keep up."

"I can help out; I can even bring a friend so you can take a break."

"What? Why would you do that?" Icelyn stood there, mouth agape, unable to process the friendly offer.

"If I help you, maybe I'll actually get the scoop over the other papers. Plus, your booth was where everything was happening. I might get a good story while I'm there."

"If you're serious, you would be a life saver. I was really worried about who to ask. Not many people really know me here, despite my living here most of my life."

"Ooh, I didn't know you were raised here?"

"My stepmother always claimed I was too much of a distraction and was better off staying home working. I wasn't allowed to go out much." Icelyn looked away; her history wasn't something she liked to share.

Tasha blinked. "That's interesting." She didn't write down anything. It appeared that Tasha was not the sort to make money on someone's personal tragedy. "Let's make a deal: As soon as you've figured out what's going on with the prince, give me an exclusive interview. In exchange, I'll bring my friend over every day during the festival and help serve your hot cocoa."

"Deal." Icelyn shook Tasha's outstretched hand. "I really should get going, I need to check on my supplies for tomorrow. Make sure I have everything."

"Okay then, I'll see you tomorrow. And hopefully soon we can sit down for an interview."

Icelyn watched as Tasha walked off, surprised but grateful that the woman was so nice. Ember flew above her as she hurried back to the shop. She had a lot to do before bed, and all she could really think about was curling up under her pink-and-teal wool blanket with Ember cuddled up behind her knees. It was a dream she intended on making come true soon.

"Holly, were you able to get the supplies?" she asked as she opened the shop door. Ember flew in, only to stop and land suddenly.

She screeched to a halt as well. Her shop was a disaster. It looked like someone had ripped apart every pillow she had in the shop. Feathers were everywhere. Her comfy chairs were slashed, the insides spilling out. This was not going to be as easy to fix as ingredients strewn all over.

This was going to be expensive, hopefully not so expensive it put her out of business.

"Oh my gods, Icelyn, what's happened here?" Holly dropped her bags at her feet.

"Another round of sabotage it would seem. I'm not sure how much more of this I can afford. Let's get everything packed for tomorrow. Hopefully I'll make enough tomorrow to cover the loss from tonight." Icelyn grabbed a broom and got to work, scared to even think about what else could happen to her during this festival.

Chapter Fourteen

The next morning Icelyn started the day even more determined to be a success, even though she wasn't able to open her shop due to all the damage from last night. Holly was certain the twins were involved. Not that Icelyn wanted to encourage Holly's war path of vengeance, but she was pretty sure it was the twins as well. Especially after that debacle at the sculpture contest. It just wasn't worth doing anything until she actually had proof. So, her plan for today was to point everyone to her festival booth, bring twice as many baked goods as yesterday, and hopefully sell out of everything, just like yesterday. Which was why the sun was just coming up, but she had been running around her kitchen for the last three hours. By the end of the festival, she might collapse from it all, but for now, she was filled with energy and excitement for whatever the day had in store for her.

Ember, on the other hand, was in her extra fluffy bed snoozing the morning . . . middle of the night . . . away.

Bursting through the door, Holly called out, "I'm here."

Ember awoke with a tiny burst of flame, followed by tiny coughs of smoke. She rubbed the sleep from her eyes, then looked at Holly like she wanted to set her on fire. Not that she ever would, but Ember was not a dragon that appreciated being woken up from a deep sleep. With a *harumph*, Ember lay back down and curled up into her bed, asleep and snoring almost as quickly as she had woken up.

"It seems Ember is not done with her beauty sleep. We can just pack her and her bed into the cart. It will give her a place to rest after the race today," Icelyn rambled as she began to gather her supplies for the day.

"Why do you seem so nervous? You smashed it yesterday. Ran out of everything. And today you're prepared for even more customers." Holly grabbed the last of the items on the counter.

Icelyn sighed. "Now I have to sell enough to get new furniture for my shop. It took me a long time to find the perfect items. I feel like I'm starting all over."

"This time you have a better chance of success. You're building a solid customer base, and I know something's going on with the prince. I don't think you need to worry about your future." Holly walked outside to finish packing the cart. Glancing back, she said, "Now, grab your sleeping dragon so we can go."

Icelyn wanted to take her time in protest but there was way too much to get done before the first customers arrived. Instead of throwing a small fit, she said a small thanks for her troublesome friend, grabbed Ember's mushing harness, and tossed it into the oversized bed Ember slept in. She grabbed the bed with all its contents and left her shop.

Holly was already sitting in the cart, ready to go. Icelyn swore she even saw her tapping her foot.

"I'm coming, I'm coming." Icelyn laid Ember and her bed in the front of the cart and scanned the goods in the back with a practiced eye. "Okay, everything looks good. Let's head to our home away from home."

The sun encouraged the sleepy town to wake up as the light filtered through the trees and buildings, causing the snow to glisten like fairy dust. Icelyn loved the magic that mornings brought with them. There was something special about the soft morning light that made her feel like every sunrise was a fresh start, a new beginning, a time to reinvest in her dreams.

Icelyn stopped the cart in front of the hot cocoa stand. "It's only been a day, but I already feel like this little outdoor kitchen is home," she said, sounding wistful as she ran her hands over the counter.

"This place is home for now, especially with your shop closed today." Holly glanced over with disdain. "We need to do something about whoever is breaking in. I mean, we can't let the twins get away with it." She jumped off the wagon, arms crossed as she turned towards Icelyn.

"I like how you went from 'we need to do something about whoever is breaking in,' to 'the twins need to be punished.' We don't actually know it's them and we can't start pointing fingers until there's proof, which we aren't going to get today." Icelyn tossed her shimmering hair over her shoulder. "In fact, I just want to forget it happened for today. Let's enjoy the customers and the crowd."

"Talk about a good time, looks like Prince Colden is on his way over," Holly teased.

"It's nothing, he just wants to get away from the mass of women and men throwing themselves at him, and I agreed to help him out." Icelyn shrugged.

Holly crossed her arms. "What exactly does that mean?"

"It just means we are helping each other out, nothing more. He's bringing attention to my shop. And I'm pretending to date him. He doesn't have any actual interest in me." She turned back to the ingredients now bubbling on the stove.

"I don't know about this plan of yours. It sounds like a good way to end up with a broken heart." Holly reached out and gave Icelyn's shoulder a squeeze.

Icelyn rolled her shoulders back. "It'll be fine, it's just business."

She handed Holly the spoon to the hot cocoa mix, stepped around to the front of the booth, and attempted to look casual as she leaned on the counter as if she was just here to talk to Holly.

"Douglas, Prince Colden, how nice to see you again," Holly exclaimed loudly, with a smile that didn't quite reach her eyes.

"Fantastic. Now, where's Ember? I'm ready for the mushing competition." Douglas's jovial spirit brought a smile to Icelyn's face. She glanced over to see Holly grinning now as well.

"Ember's still asleep in the cart. Resting for her big day," she said, pointing to a fluffy bed with a purple dragon curled up in it like a vibrant cinnamon roll.

Icelyn watched as the prince followed her friend's flirtation with his captain of the guard, his gaze shifting back and forth as they spoke.

"You're here a lot," Colden said.

"Yep, just helping my friend out. Her shop was ransacked last night. She needed someone to open for her while she catalogued all the damage."

"Do you have time for a sleigh ride today, Icelyn?" the prince asked with a slight nod.

Icelyn glanced around, hoping to see Tasha and her friend nearby. "I'm not sure, I should probably get back to my shop soon, before it gets too busy for my assistant to handle on her own."

"Nothing is going to get busy until the dragon mushing race starts, and that isn't for a few hours. I'm sure your . . . assistant . . . can handle it until help arrives. Go now. They'll learn everything they need to know before the race. Who knows, maybe you'll even be back by then?" Holly chimed in, pushing her and the prince away from the hot cocoa booth.

"Are you sure, Holly? Some of the things still need to be finished before the shop opens." Icelyn looked around, noticing all the work that needed to be done.

"I'm sure your assistant will take care of it until reinforcements show up, and then we'll head out to the mushing race with Ember." Holly shoved Icelyn towards the prince.

Icelyn turned to the prince. "I have a few things I need to take care of before I can enjoy any excursion. Why don't we meet by the gazebo in half an hour."

"Of course, I don't want to be a distraction—well, at least not too much of a distraction." His arm slid around her waist, pulling her until they were touching each other from chest to thigh. She felt her cheeks, no, her entire body heat up. He used his other hand to tilt her head up until she was looking him in his icy-blue eyes. He leaned in and . . . kissed her cheek. A sigh of disappointment escaped before she could stop it. Colden dropped his arm as he took a step back, a rakish grin making him even more handsome. "See you in a bit." With a quick wave, he turned and walked away.

Icelyn looked around. "Okay, okay, just give me a moment to finish this and I'll be ready to go."

"We have this . . ." Icelyn stopped Holly with a look.

It wasn't long before Icelyn had finished the cocoa for the day, ensuring that there was a bit of magic in every ounce. Just enough to make everyone that tried a sip happy. Icelyn tasted a sip and sighed contentedly. The s'more mixture was exactly how she had envisioned it.

Holly interrupted her satisfied thoughts. "You better go. You wouldn't want to keep the prince waiting."

"You're right. I need to run." Icelyn grabbed her cloak and ran through town, nearly knocking a few people over along the way.

"I'm ready. Where are we off to?" she asked, gulping in air to catch her breath after her sprint across town.

"I thought a nice ride through the woods and town would be fun, before you're too busy." Prince

Colden offered Icelyn his arm, kindly ignoring her panting.

She tossed her hair back and laughed. "Fine, let's go. But I want to be back in time for Ember's mushing competition. I don't want to miss my baby girl in her meet." She took Colden's arm and let him escort her to the sleigh, and what a sleigh it was. Shiny blue and silver coated the vehicle, black runners seemed to hover over the snow, and the dappled grey horses pulling it were two of the most magnificent creatures she had ever seen.

Colden helped her up into the sleigh then took the seat beside her. Grabbing the reins, he clicked his tongue, and they were off. The wintry air caressed her cheek, causing a shiver to make its way down her spine. She felt Colden wrap his arm around her as she pulled the wool blankets close to her body. For the moment, she was content to sit here in silence, watching the sleepy town wake up before her eyes as the sleigh carved its way through the almost empty streets on its way to the surrounding forest.

The other festival booths were filling up as they rode by, reminding her she needed to make the time to stop by and support other local businesses. She shivered again, her knit hat was no match for the breeze of the carriage. Colden pulled her in closer, and she was tempted to burrow into his arms further to stay warm. But looking around, she could see everyone staring. Including Maude and the twins. Their glares held her in place until they were out of town.

"Are you okay?" Colden asked as the sleigh entered onto a forest path. He slowed the horses to a trot, allowing her to focus on the beauty of the snow-dusted evergreens around her, instead of the evil glares of her family.

"Yes, it's just the twins; they seem to notice every time we are together, and they are always up to no good. I think . . ." Icelyn shook her head ever so slightly. "Never mind, it's not important. No need to let talk of the twins ruin a good time."

"If you're sure, but I can help if you want me to. Just say the word," Colden offered. It reminded her how much he really could do as a prince and future king,

"I would rather handle it myself. There's no need for you to step in yet. If I do need help, I'll let you know." Icelyn snuggled into his warmth. "Since we are out here with no one chasing after you, tell me something about yourself."

"My favorite color is blue. And I prefer hot cocoa to coffee," Colden offered.

"Not something so unimportant, although I agree hot cocoa is the superior hot drink. I want to know something about you no one else knows." Icelyn crossed her arms. "And everyone knows your favorite color is blue. Your sleigh is blue, you wear almost exclusively blue. I figured you were just being vain and trying to bring out the color of your eyes."

"So, you've noticed the color of my eyes, have you? Does that mean you like them? Maybe even find me handsome?"

"Fishing for compliments is beneath you, Your Highness. And a terrible way to avoid my question."

Colden sighed. "Something serious, huh? Well, I don't feel ready to get married. I always wanted to marry for love, but my father placed this deadline on finding my soulmate. Which is impossible to do. And while I know that person is out there, the pressure of finding them in such a short period makes me want to run and hide."

"Have you told your father any of this?"

"Yes, but he thinks I need to have a partner to be able to rule. Maybe he's right, but I think I'm capable on my own. Not only capable but ready. If he will ever retire."

"Is he planning on stepping down?"

"He says so, when he feels like I'm ready. But how will he know if he never involves me in royal business?"

"Again, have you talked to him about any of this?"

"I've tried, but it hasn't done any good." Colden shrugged.

"Maybe you need to insist instead of ask."

Colden opened his mouth to respond but the pounding of hooves interrupted his thoughts. He stopped the sleigh just as Douglas and Holly burst onto the path. They came to a halt in front of them.

"Icelyn, it's Ember. We were doing a practice run to warm up and her harness broke. I don't know where she flew off to." Holly gasped for air in between sobs. "I'm so sorry, Ember is missing."

Icelyn's eyes darted between her friend and the prince. Her heart, her pet dragon, was missing. It couldn't be true. Tears welled in her eyes before overflowing. "Take me back. Now."

Chapter Fifteen

Colden watched as Icelyn sat down beside him. Tears froze on her face as she huddled into the corner of the carriage seat, her arms crossed, creating a wall between them. He wanted to comfort her, but he didn't know how to. Especially since everything her body said indicated he should stay away. So, he sat there silently despite feeling a desperate need to make her feel better. A feeling that was something new for him.

"Icelyn . . ." He paused, not sure what else to say. "Is there anything I can do to help?"

"No. I never should have left. I knew better." She sniffed.

Colden glanced in her direction. "What do you mean, you knew better?"

"It's nothing. This is just how my life goes, and right now I'm being targeted more than ever before."

Colden made eye contact with Douglas, raising an eyebrow as he did so. He wanted to know if this was happening, and if it was, why didn't he already know about it? When Douglas looked over, he nodded yes. The instant affirmation had Colden fuming. Why did he not know anything about this? Part of this deal was helping Icelyn out, and he couldn't do it if he didn't know what was going on. The look he gave Douglas clearly indicated that a talk would be happening in the very near future.

The ride back to town continued in silence. Icelyn blocked herself off from everyone, the turmoil she felt apparent in every single one of her movements. Colden watched as she refused to look at everyone, especially him. But it was more than that: she wouldn't look at her friend Holly either. Holly kept trying to get her attention as they rode back to town.

As soon as he stopped the carriage, Icelyn jumped out. Colden watched as Holly scurried after her, the two of them stopping on the stoop in front of Icelyn's cottage. He stood there contemplating his best course of action, deciding it was time to talk to Douglas, at least for now. He needed more information.

"Douglas! Wait, let Holly and Icelyn figure out what they are going to do to find Ember. While they plan, why don't you tell me what's been going on? Why does everyone think she's being targeted? And why don't I know anything about it?" Colden paced, his cloak floating behind him in the breeze.

"Ever since you started talking to her, Icelyn's shop has been the target of multiple incidents. I've been able to handle them myself—using your name. Not that Icelyn knows that. She wants to fix everything herself. She doesn't want you to know. She barely allowed me to help. And she won't let Holly or me go after the culprits, even though we are certain we know who they are." Douglas threw up his hands, frustrated by everything. "She's a stubborn one, that's for sure. And takes on a lot of the blame herself. If Ember doesn't turn up, she's not going to be okay. That little dragon means the world to her. She got her when she moved out of her stepmother's house. Ember's been her constant companion since she decided to go at it alone."

"Who's doing this to her?" Colden asked.

Douglas looked at the prince as if he was intentionally oblivious. "It's obvious if you took half a second to think about it. Who threw a fit at the snow sculpture contest yesterday? Oh, and are those the same people that throw themselves at your feet any time they have a chance? If you don't already know the answer, it is yes. Yes, they are the same people."

"I get it, but did you really have to be so snarky about it?" Colden stopped. "So, the twins are bothering her."

" 'Bothering her' would be putting it lightly. So far, they've destroyed everything she needs to make the goods she sells. I was able to fix that by getting her a line of credit with all the merchants. No one would give her one before because she's a new business and Maude was threatening all of them," Douglas explained.

"What does Maude have to do with her not getting lines of credit?"

"Oh Colden, it's like you live in a castle on a hill far away, and don't know about anything that happens here in town," Douglas said with a laugh.

"Yeah, yeah. I'm removed from everything." Colden crossed his arms. "But that's why I have you, and why you have Holly. Hanging around her has to help you get all the information I don't have."

"It's true, you don't have a Holly to help you out. She's very well informed about Icelyn's life. Holly was Icelyn's only friend growing up. From what I've heard, Icelyn did not have an easy childhood. But that's her story to tell, not mine."

"I don't want to pry into her life, ask her for any more than she's willing to give. But I do need to know more about what the twins are doing. I could stop it." Colden swiped his hand through his hair, leaving every hair in disarray.

Douglas grabbed Colden. "Listen, she doesn't want you to fix it. That's why she hasn't told you. So far, I've been able to help without getting overly involved. Right now, her shop is closed because she needs all new furniture after the last attack. But that's nothing compared to Ember being missing. She loves that dragon more than life itself. If we don't find her, I'm not sure she'll recover. Focus on that, and let her figure out what to do about the twins' actions."

"You're right, respecting boundaries. If she wants my help, she'll ask. Until then, let's focus on finding Ember."

Colden made his way to where Icelyn and Holly were searching. He didn't make it far though; he heard his name called over by the hot cocoa booth. With a sigh, he turned to address whoever was calling him.

"Prince Colden, can I have a moment?" Tasha asked while waving him over to the booth.

Colden was surprised to see her standing behind the booth, serving. It wasn't like her to be a part of the event. She normally just reported on it. It looked like she had a friend with her as well, someone he didn't recognize. Maybe she was new to town?

"What can I help you with, Tasha?" he asked as he approached the booth.

"I wanted the scoop on you and Icelyn. She won't tell me anything. But I can tell there's something happening between the two of you. It's all the town can talk about, and I have nothing to report." She put her hands on her hips.

"Is this really the place to talk business? You have a line to take care of." Colden pointed to the line forming behind her.

Tasha turned and gasped. "Envi," she pointed to the line, "do you think you can handle this?"

Envi looked up, her blue eyes wide. She wiped her black bangs off her pale forehead and sighed. "I've got this, Tasha, but you owe me."

"I know, I know. But you know I'm the best person to help get your business off the ground so it will be worth it." Tasha patted her friend on the shoulder. "Okay, Prince Colden, what's the scoop?"

"The scoop is that Icelyn's shop has been targeted multiple times by someone in town. This last time, they destroyed everything, including her furniture. She had to shut down the shop because everything was damaged. As a new business, she can't afford to get new furniture, even though she's a vendor at the festival. It's not enough for her to repurchase everything." Colden clasped his hands behind his back as the two of them walked.

"Why don't you just buy her all new things?" Tasha asked.

"I would if she'd let me. She's agreed to date me, but she's incredibly hesitant to ask for my help. She doesn't want anyone to think she's using me. Or even worse, she didn't earn her place here at the festival."

"I can see her dilemma, but I do think there's something that I can do to help. Did you just confirm that you and Icelyn are dating? Does that mean you are officially off the market? The entire town wants to know." Tasha tapped her pencil on her notebook.

"For now, we are seeing where things go, but I have a good feeling about it," Colden said before muttering something under his breath.

"What was that?"

"Nothing, I don't mind the relationship being in the paper. But I'm worried it will cause Icelyn even more problems. At the moment, we are searching for her dragon, because she broke loose right before the mushing competition during the practice run."

"Ember's missing, and you're talking to me? You have to go find her. That dragon is so important to Icelyn. I barely know her and even I know that." Tasha shoved the prince towards the path where Icelyn and Holly were walking.

"That's what I was doing before someone interrupted me," Colden said over his shoulder as he made his way to Icelyn's side.

Chapter Sixteen

"It's all my fault, Holly," Icelyn said between sniffles. "I didn't check her harness. If I had been here, I would have checked and made sure everything was in good condition, and Ember would still be here safe with me. I should have never gone on the carriage ride with the prince."

Holly pulled Icelyn in for a hug, causing even more tears to flow. "It's not your fault. I should have checked her equipment better."

"Oh Holly, I would never blame you for any of this. It was so nice of you to enter the contest for me. This is all my fault."

Icelyn heard someone clear their voice. She turned to see Douglas there holding the harness. It was sliced almost all the way through right where the harness connected to the mushing lines. She stared at the damage, the intentional damage, and knew this was just another thing the twins had done.

"I'm going to kill them. Why are they doing this to me?" Icelyn turned away from Holly and Douglas to see Colden approach. "It's because of you."

She watched him stop in his tracks. Colden's jaw dropped as he stared at her, clearly not expecting her accusation.

"If I hadn't been out with you, this never would have happened. I would have been there, I would have noticed the broken harness, and Ember would still be here." She wiped tears from her cheeks. "I should have never gotten involved with you."

"Icelyn, I'm sure Ember is fine. We can work together to find her." Colden reached out to her, but she stepped away before he could touch her.

"No, I can't. I need some space. And I need my dragon. I don't have time for you right now." Before she could say anything else she knew she would eventually regret, she walked away, leaving the prince standing there completely befuddled.

Icelyn avoided making eye contact with anyone as she walked through town back to her shop, tears constantly streaming down her face. She didn't even know where to look for Ember and the overwhelming sense of helplessness was consuming her. Everything was a blur until she stood in front of her shop door. She hoped Ember would be there, curled up asleep on the step after an exciting adventure. But her purple dragon wasn't there. Fumbling with her keys, the blinding tears making it a struggle to unlock the door, she must have dropped them half a dozen times before she finally got the key into the keyhole. The door opened; she stepped through and closed the door behind her, then slid to the floor, desolate.

There was a knock on the door that was currently supporting her back. She sighed and scootched across the floor so the door could open.

"Icelyn, it's Holly, can I come in?"

"It's open."

Holly pushed open the door until it hit Icelyn's foot. "Okay sweetie, you can't just lie on the floor." She held her hand out to Icelyn. "The prince and Douglas are out searching for Ember. Why don't you go to the kitchen and figure out what you are going to serve tomorrow?"

"I don't know, I should be out searching." She sniffed.

"No, you stay here, there's enough people searching. And Ember might come here on her own. You should be here if she does." Holly led her to the kitchen.

"I guess you're right." Icelyn walked into her happy space feeling anything but happy. What she felt was extreme loss. She walked around the kitchen gathering butter, sugar, salt, vanilla, and other necessary ingredients for the salted caramel cocoa that had been floating around in her head.

She started with sugar, lots of sugar, pouring it into a pan and setting it over the fire to melt, starting the process of perfect caramel making. She watched as the powder turned into a liquid and slowly started to brown. When the liquid was the perfect rich amber color, she took the cream she had set close to the fire to warm it and poured it into the sugar. She stirred as fast as she could until the bubbling stopped. As soon as she slowed down, thoughts of Ember overtook her, and a single tear fell into the mixture. She covered up her mixture for tomorrow.

"Holly, let's go to the cottage. Ember is just as likely to go there as she is here." Icelyn said, her movements mechanical as she gathered her things.

"If that's what you want. It's not like it's a far walk."

Icelyn almost smiled at that. She'd bought the small cottage next to the shop. She had plans for the upstairs of the shop and didn't want her needing it for home to interfere with them.

Holly held the door open for her as Icelyn shuffled her way through. Every movement seemed to take so much energy. It was like all her energy was focused on her concern for Ember, and her body barely had enough left to function.

"Come on, let's get you settled in front of the fire while Douglas and Colden are out looking for Ember. You know you'll feel better at home, with a drink. I'm just going to take a mug of this and add a bit of whiskey to it for you." Holly made sure Icelyn settled in her home before disappearing for a few minutes. When she returned, she had a piping hot mug of cocoa with her. "Drink this. It will help you relax."

Icelyn took a sip, staring into the fire as she did so. She felt tears slide down her cheeks as she thought about her little dragon out there all alone in the cold.

A loud bang snapped her out of her morose musings. "What the . . .," she muttered. Tossing her blanket to the side, she stood and made her way to the front door. She heard the rumbling voice of Douglas and the more clipped tones of the prince, and—did she hear toe tapping, wings flapping? Could they have found her baby girl? Her pace quickened as she let herself feel hope for the first time since Holly told her Ember was missing. She threw the door open to see everyone standing around. Holly kept picking up Ember and hugging her as tears streamed down her face. Both men smiled broadly, clearly proud of their accomplishment.

"Oh Ember, I'm so happy to see you. What did you end up doing today?" Icelyn held her arms open, and her dragon half flew, half ran to her. Icelyn's tears turned to tears of joy.

"Where were you today, little one?" Icelyn asked.

Colden cleared his throat. "Well, you see, Ember was curled up at your front door. You would have found her soon enough."

Icelyn locked eyes with Colden. After what she said earlier, it surprised her that he was so honest. He didn't try to take credit for finding

Ember to earn her forgiveness. Forgiveness he didn't really need because none of this was his fault. She should apologize to him for earlier, but she wasn't ready. Since they met, it felt like she was being targeted. Still, she felt guilt creep in as she thought back to her earlier outburst. She looked up at the prince.

"It's okay, Icelyn. It sorta was my fault. Ember wasn't the only one with the sabotaged harness. Half the dragons flew away today during the race. Then there were the branches that fell during the snow sculpture contest. I'm worried someone is trying to ruin the festival this year." He bowed and left. Leaving Icelyn there crying over the return of Ember, and maybe the loss of the prince.

Chapter Seventeen

"I feel terrible. Since Icelyn met me so much has happened to her. The two break-ins and Ember going missing. I'm afraid knowing me is hurting her more than it is helping her. And I want to change that if I can." Colden paced the length of his room, stopping periodically to include Douglas in the conversation. However, he never stopped long enough for Douglas to actually speak.

Colden continued to wear a hole in his carpet as he tried to figure out what to do. He wanted to help Icelyn. He liked her, liked listening to her insights about the town and its people. But it felt like he was doing more harm than good.

"Colden, why don't you do something nice for Icelyn? A gift of some sort. I know you want to do more, but anything other than a nice gesture could upset her. She wants to handle her problems herself, in her own way," Douglas said.

"I wish I could take care of the twins; someone needs to put them in their place. Unfortunately, I should respect her wishes. So, I'm going to try to do just that."

"You do need to respect her wishes. She's already on edge. She feels like only bad things have happened since you two have met. But that doesn't mean you can't help in other ways."

Colden raised an eyebrow. "What do you have in mind?"

Douglas rubbed his hands together conspiratorially. "I have a few ideas. But are you sure that's what you want to focus on? You mentioned all the harnesses were damaged before the race. That can't be good for the rest of the festival."

The prince sank down into his chair. "I know that's what I should be focused on, but I can't stop thinking about Icelyn and the damage to her store." Colden shook his head. "But you're right. The festival is my priority. It needs to be a success, and so far, one event was almost ruined, and the dragon mushing . . . Well, you know what happened there."

"I don't understand why anyone would do anything to harm the Snow Solstice Festival. It does so much good for the town. I don't think it could be anyone in town."

"It would be strange if it was someone in town. The first festival victims were the twins, so it probably isn't related to whatever they have against Icelyn. Even though they didn't take any time in blaming Icelyn for it. It could be some really complicated and convoluted plot." Colden crossed his legs as he leaned back in the chair. He steepled his fingers under his chin, deep in thought. "We need to be on guard at the next events, hire more people, keep an eye out for anyone acting suspicious, report back with anything that you find."

"I can do that. I'll arrange for more guards at the ice maze opening tomorrow. We don't need to have any problems."

"Perfect. Now back to your ideas to help out Icelyn."

"It's less about helping her and more about a grand gesture."

Colden looked over, his eyes full of skepticism. "What do you mean . . . grand gesture?"

"Were you planning on taking her to the Ice Masquerade Ball?" Douglas asked.

Colden sighed. "I was thinking about it, but I don't want to cause any more trouble."

"Do you like her?"

"Of course, I like her, that's why I'm spending time with her," Colden responded with a scoff.

"That's not what I mean. Do you like, like her? Could she be the one for you?" Douglas sat forward in his chair waiting for the prince to respond.

"I don't know, I like being around her, it's easy for the most part. She sees the world so differently; it's eye opening. But right now, she's just doing me a favor, and I'm trying to return it by helping her shop. You have that taken care of, right?" Colden sat back in his chair. "I do like her, but there's also the hot cocoa maker. I desperately want to meet them."

"Don't you want to know what you're doing to help her business, or at least what her business is? It might help clarify a few things for you." Douglas tried to get him to ask more questions about Icelyn.

"No, just as long as it's being done. That's what matters. Now, if I were to invite her to the Ice Masquerade Ball, what sorta grand gesture were you thinking?"

Douglas leapt up from the chair. "It's time we go shopping."

"Did I really have to come down and do this? I hate shopping," Colden whined in a way only a prince could whine.

"Yes, it's a grand gesture. It has to actually come from you." Douglas dragged the prince to one of the new dress shops. "What you should do is buy her a dress for the event. She's invested everything she owns into her business. So, if you invite her to go, she might say no because she can't find anything to wear. But if you send her something to wear with the invite, I bet she shows up."

Before Colden could respond, he was ambushed by the twins, Stacey with her bouncy ringlet curls and Dru in his typical fuchsia coat barreled towards him and practically screeched to a halt in front of him.

"Your Highness, how good it is to see you again." Stacey all but fell as she attempted a curtsy.

"Did I just hear that you are planning to go to the ball?" Dru asked, but continued on before the prince could respond. "Who's the lucky person?"

They both attempted to grab his arms and escort him away from Douglas, but one glare from the lumberjack of a man had them stopping in their tracks. Colden almost burst out laughing as he watched them stop mid-shenanigan. His never-ending training for state dinners serving a purpose for once.

"Anyway, I must be off. I need to get some important things done before tomorrow." With a dismissive bow, Colden turned and left the twins standing there, hoping they would be deterred by his lack of interest. Instead, the two followed him as he and Douglas went from shop to shop looking for the perfect gift for Icelyn. Nothing seemed to be right, even though each shop had wonderful items, but nothing for the ball, and nothing that seemed to fit what he knew about her.

"I don't know what we're looking for, Douglas, but it doesn't seem like we are going to find it. How many shops have we been to so far?" Colden gestured at the rows of shops and booths that lined the cobblestone streets.

"Someone will have the perfect thing to give to Icelyn as part of her invite to the ball."

Colden heard a gasp behind him. He turned just in time to see a flash of fuchsia cut between two of the marketplace shops.

"Dammit, I think the twins heard us. What if they do something more to make her life harder? I should go after them." Colden took a few steps after them, but stopped when Douglas grabbed his shoulder.

"She doesn't want you to confront them. I'll keep my eyes out. Try to make sure nothing else happens," Douglas said.

"Okay . . . for now." Colden turned to look inside the next shop. And once again it came up short. Nothing spoke to him. He sighed as disappointment set in. This was never going to work.

That's when he saw it. The perfect gown for Icelyn to wear to the ball. It was all the colors of her hair in one spectacular ballgown. He stopped and just stared at the dress. He loved how the embroidered flowers sprinkled down the dress as if it was raining flowers, and how the iridescent fabric captured them before they hit the ground. There was a gorgeous pair of skates next to it.

They were also iridescent, almost crystal looking, with flowers that matched the dress. He could see her twirling on the ice in the dress, looking like the magical person she was.

"Douglas, this is it," Colden said as he ran his hands over the fabric. The fabric was silky to the touch.

"Are you sure it's not too much for Icelyn? She seems to like staying a bit more in the shadows than she would be able to do in that dress." Douglas looked at the dress with a critical eye.

"True, but she would be a vision in this dress." Colden caressed the dress once again. "No, I'm not going to look for anything else. This dress is the one."

"Okay, I'll go make all the arrangements to have it delivered."

"Thank you, Douglas, I don't know what I would do without you."

"Very little, I'm sure," Douglas muttered.

Chapter Eighteen

The caramel and cocoa were packed, Ember was asleep in the cart, and Holly was bundled up behind the reins, ready to head to the booth by the ice maze. Icelyn was excited to serve the salted caramel hot cocoa. It was one of her most popular recipes, or at least it would be if more people came to the café regularly. On top of that, today was most people's favorite day of the festival. The ice maze was always a huge draw, bringing people to Wynterfell from neighboring towns. Everyone's excitement was one of the things she looked forward to. She hoped today was as busy as it was every other year.

"Come on, Icelyn, I'm freezing up here. Stop your lollygagging around," Holly hollered at her.

"I'm coming, I'm coming." She locked the café door with a slight smile. Today she felt lighter than she had for some time. Ember finding her way home yesterday was such a relief it made today feel brighter. Humming a winter song, she hopped into the cart with a little extra spring in her step.

"What has you so peppy today?" Holly asked as the cart started to move towards town.

"I don't know, I just feel good today. Despite all the crap that's been happening around here, today is a new day. I'm selling my hot cocoa to the town. It's the day of the ice maze. What's there not to be peppy about?" Icelyn flipped up the collar of her coat as the wind picked up.

"True. I'm used to everything weighing on you just a little bit more, but I'm thrilled to see it not. It does seem like today is going to be a fantastic day, if we can both keep a cheerful outlook."

"And why shouldn't we! It's a good day."

They made their way through town until they were at the stand outside of the ice maze. The maze glistened with the light of the rising sun. The snow-covered walls were decorated with blue bows and silver bunting, giving the entire area a magically festive feeling.

Icelyn jumped out of the cart, stretched, and unpacked her things for the day. Holly took Ember and her bed and made sure she was settled behind the counter. Icelyn smiled seeing her dragon settle, started the stove fire, and got to work. She danced around the stall as she warmed up all her ingredients for today's hot cocoa, starting with the milk and chocolate, then the salted caramel she made the day before. Holly helped her assemble the drinks, drizzling caramel and chocolate around the inside of the cups, pouring the hot liquid in, adding dollops of whipped cream, more caramel, and a sprinkle of salt to finish it off. It was a work of art.

Icelyn wrote the day's menu on the board, including Fireside Nap, her salted caramel concoction.

As soon as she was done, the line started forming. She smiled as she went to the counter to start taking orders.

"Hi, Danny! How are the kids? Are they enjoying the festival?" Icelyn asked one of her new regulars. He had come to her cart every day of the festival, and always tried the special of the day and one of her baked goods. "Do you want the special today?"

"Of course, it's been a delicious adventure trying all of your drink concoctions. Plus, I have to try your winterberry croissant. That looks amazing. The kids are good, they are super excited about the maze today."

"You're too sweet, Danny." Icelyn grabbed his order. "Here you go. Say hi to your little ones for me."

"Of course. See you tomorrow."

The morning continued with friendly customers coming and going, the majority ordering the Fireside Nap. It thrilled Icelyn to see so many people enjoying her creations.

"Icelyn, something is happening," Holly said slowly.

"What do you mean?" Icelyn asked, confusion tingeing her tone.

"Look around, why is everyone crying?" Holly asked. "Look, there's Danny with his kids. Tears are streaming down his face, just like everyone else that ordered the caramel hot cocoa."

Icelyn felt her palms start to sweat and her heart race. This wasn't good. No one wanted to feel sad, they wanted to feel happy and loved. She tried so hard to only cook when she felt those emotions. Yesterday, she made the caramel while Ember was missing. While she was feeling both extreme love and sadness. Hopefully, it wasn't just sadness that everyone was feeling, and she hoped it didn't last long.

Icelyn looked around town. Tears were falling down almost everyone's face. "Oh no, this isn't good at all," Icelyn said, her eyes affixed on the crowd.

"I knew you had magic." Holly clapped her hands together, more excited than concerned at the prospect of Icelyn's drink causing everyone to cry.

"And it's making everyone cry. It's not good. I normally control it better than this." Icelyn thrummed her fingers on the counter.

"Stop worrying and look around again. Don't focus on what you think is bad and really take it all in." Holly turned Icelyn to the crowd, forcing her to really look.

Some people were crying, but now most were laughing and dancing. The tears from before had morphed into something different, something joyful. Icelyn let out the breath she was holding, relieved that her magic had created something more complex than sadness. People will remember today being a great day. They won't ever make the connection between her hot cocoa and how they felt today.

"What a relief. I thought the café was done for."

"Why didn't you ever tell me you had magic? I always said you did, but you never confirmed it." Holly crossed her arms in a huff.

"Because . . . I don't know . . . It's just not something I've ever shared. It just makes me even weirder than I already am. And I get tired of feeling like I don't belong." Icelyn shrugged and turned back to the stove.

"But it's me. I wouldn't have thought anything of it. Well, I would have thought it was awesome. What does your magic do?" Holly leaned in.

"It's not that impressive. People just feel whatever I feel while I'm cooking, so it's a good thing I am always happiest when I'm making something."

Icelyn turned to look at the townsfolk again. Everyone was happy, everyone but Dru and Stacey. They stood by the maze, staring at her booth with contempt. Icelyn looked away, wondering what those two would do next.

"Holly, can you handle the booth for a bit? I need to see if I can find the prince, apologize for yesterday." Icelyn wiped her hands on her apron before taking it off.

Holly looked at the line that had dwindled to only a few people and turned back to Icelyn. "Go, take your time. Maybe explore the maze with him. Envi and Tasha will be back soon."

"Thank you, I really appreciate you," Icelyn said before making her way to the front of the maze where a burly redheaded guard stood tall. "Douglas, is Colden around today?"

"That depends. Are you going to yell at him and make him feel bad again?"

"No, I actually want to apologize. I was out of line yesterday." Icelyn averted her eyes and blushed.

"In that case, he's at the front of the maze, just after the first left turn."

Icelyn waved goodbye to Douglas and made her way towards the maze. It had been years since she had experienced the ice maze. Her last experience didn't leave her feeling very confident. It was right after her father had married Maude. The twins had agreed to spend the day with her at the festival. They took her to the maze, promising an adventure, but ran as soon as they were far enough in to make it a challenge to get out no matter which way she went. It took her hours to find her way out, and when she returned home, Maude had yelled at her for disappearing for the day and sent her to the cellar. She had avoided this particular event ever since, until today.

She took a deep breath and rolled her shoulders back before she took the step into the maze. She went in and turned right the first place she had a choice of where to go. Her feet slowed as she got farther into the maze and didn't see Colden. The next two turns only offered one direction, towards the right. She was on edge, feeling like her first choice was the wrong one, and she needed to start over. She was about to do just that when she heard her name.

"Icelyn, is that you?" the prince asked.

She turned towards his voice, a smile stretched out across her face. "Hi, Colden, what a surprise to find you here."

"You are?"

"Honestly, no. I'm not surprised. I asked Douglas where you were." She blushed.

"Why?"

"I see you aren't going to make this easy on me. I want to apologize for yesterday: I should have never blamed you. It's not your fault someone sabotaged the event. It's the fault of the saboteur." Icelyn drew circles in the snow with her foot.

"I appreciate your apology. But I feel like I should have done something. The whole thing was a disaster, but it could have been so much worse. At least no one was injured or lost for long. But I feel terrible for everyone that was worried about their dragon." Colden moved closer to her.

She remembered how it felt to be cuddled up next to him during their sleigh ride.

"It's kind of you to care so much about everyone." She took a step back, her back hitting the wall of ice and snow that created the maze.

Colden leaned in, putting one gloved hand on the wall above her head. "So, you think that I'm kind."

Icelyn licked her lower lip. "You know that I do. I wouldn't have agreed to spend time with you if I didn't think you were nice." She reached up and brushed a lock of hair off his forehead, and her hand fell to his shoulder.

"I'm not sure that's a good description of my princely personality." He reached around her waist with one hand and cupped her face with the other. "What will happen if other kingdoms think I'm nice."

She leaned in on her toes, their faces inches apart. All it would take for their lips to meet would be Colden lowering his head towards hers. If she could close the distance, she would. But she wasn't tall enough to make it happen.

"I wouldn't know what the other kingdoms would do, just what I would do," Icelyn whispered.

"Hmm," Colden hummed. "And what would you do?"

"Well, if you were nice, you would kiss me, and I would kiss back."

"Is that so?"

"Yes."

He lowered his head and pressed his lips to hers. A tingle started in the pit of her stomach and spread through the rest of her body. The kiss was a melding of their lips, nothing more, and it left her wanting.

"You call that a kiss?" She grabbed the back of his head, her fingers tangling in his hair, and pulled his head towards hers. Their lips met. Her tongue swiped across his lower lip. She felt his mouth open slightly and took that as an invitation to plunder. It wasn't long before he joined her in an intricate dance of lips, tongues, and teeth. She broke off the kiss.

"Now if only I can find someone to escort me out of the maze." Icelyn looked up at Colden and winked.

He took Icelyn by the arm and showed her the way out. The two of them chatted about anything and everything on their walk through the maze. When they exited, Icelyn was sad to see the prince go; this interlude was the cherry on the top of an already exceptional day.

"Today was good, but such a long day," Icelyn said as she packed the last of her materials back in the cart.

"I'm ready to put my feet up and relax. The booth was busy all day, even more so when you consider all the emotions of the customers today." Holly jumped up into the cart. "I can't believe you sold out of everything again. You keep making more and selling all of it. You have to be exhausted."

"I am, but I need to prepare for tomorrow. There's still a lot to do tonight," Icelyn said, but the skip in her step belayed something different.

"You always have so much to do. One day you're going to need to take a break."

"One day, but that day is not today." Icelyn laughed. She wasn't good at slowing down and her friend knew that.

"Douglas! What are you doing here?" Holly exclaimed as they arrived at the café. She jumped down from the cart and threw herself at him. Icelyn watched as he caught her friend with one arm, the other holding a package.

Icelyn took her time unhitching the horses and taking them to the stable before interrupting Douglas and Holly. "If you two want, you can come inside. I'll get a fire going and Douglas can let us know why he's here."

Douglas set Holly down and shifted the package to his now empty arm. Icelyn held the door open for her friends, then nodded towards Ember, letting the dragon know it was time to come in. Icelyn laid out some blankets and floor pillows around the fireplace; she didn't have the funds to replace the damaged chairs yet, but this was a cozy way to spend an evening, so she wasn't going to complain.

"I'm here to relay a message from the prince," Douglas said.

"Oh really." Icelyn got up to make everyone a drink.

"First, he, the prince that is, wants to apologize for what happened with Ember. He feels terrible about everything that's happened and wishes he could do something to help. I told him that you were handling it in your own way," Douglas explained, not mentioning the package that had Icelyn's curiosity piqued.

"He knows he's forgiven. In fact, I forgave him yesterday. I just wasn't ready to say anything."

"I figured as much. I couldn't help but notice the huge grin on his face when the two of you walked out of the maze together. Just a warning: the twins saw it as well. But I'm here on a different mission. If you're interested in finding out what it is."

"How exciting, I wonder what it is? Go on." Icelyn waited.

"The prince would like you to accompany him to the Ice Masquerade Ball tomorrow evening."

"Look around, I can't go." Icelyn's arm swept around the room. "I don't have anything to wear, and I can't afford to get anything."

"I think if you look at this package, you will see the prince has thought of everything." Douglas handed Icelyn a large silver box wrapped in a gorgeous red ribbon.

She sat the box on a table and carefully undid the bow. Icelyn couldn't remember the last time she opened a gift this pretty, probably before her father brought Maude into their lives. She removed the lid with care and unfolded the fabric covering the dress inside. Upon seeing the dress, she gasped. It was the most beautiful dress she had ever laid eyes on. It was iridescent, shimmering from purple to pink to blue as the light hit it from different angles.

"Icelyn, you have to try it on." Holly shooed her to the back room.

Holly wasn't the only one dying to see the dress on; Icelyn had never held anything so beautiful, and she was going to get to wear it to the ball. She shook her head in disbelief. For a moment she just stood there, in the back room, holding the dress up to her. Imagining what it would be like to wear something so pretty. When she suddenly snapped out of her haze, she disrobed, shimmied into the dress, then called Holly to help lace her into the corseted bodice.

"Oh my gods, this is the most beautiful dress I've ever seen." Holly's jaw about hit the floor when she walked in.

"Lace me in. I want to see the full effect." Icelyn giggled.

"Did you just giggle? I don't think I've ever heard that sound come from you."

"I don't think I've ever felt more like a princess, and I'm only trying the dress on. Can you imagine what it's going to feel like tomorrow?"

"Okay, I'm done."

Icelyn turned to look at herself in the mirror. The heart-shaped neckline of the fitted bodice was perfect, along with the embroidered winter flowers all over the bodice and the underskirt. The details were almost overwhelming. The top skirts shimmered from one color to the next in the light, as did the sleeves, which were made from the same fabric. It was so delicate Icelyn was surprised it kept her warm, but it did somehow. Winter flowers cascaded down the front of the overskirts where they opened to show off the gorgeous underskirt. And everything stopped mid-calf, perfect for ice skating. She was going to be able to skate to her heart's content without worrying about ruining the dress. Icelyn spun, watching the skirts swirl around her, changing colors as they did so.

"Did you see what else is in the box?" Holly asked.

"There can't be more. This is already too much."

Holly held out a matching mask and a matching pair of ice skates. The boots almost looked like glass they shimmered so much, but they were covered with the same delicate embroidery of the bodice. They were magical.

"Everything is so amazing. I shouldn't accept the gifts." Icelyn held up her hand to stop Holly from interrupting. "But I'm going to. I'm going to let myself feel like a princess for one night. Forget about all my worries and just enjoy the ball."

Chapter Nineteen

Icelyn wiped her hands on her apron after a long day at the festival. Today had been her best day yet. She had made Winter's Love, a strawberry white-chocolate cocoa for the daytime events. It had sold out faster than any other, despite her making twice as much than the day before. It felt like she couldn't prepare enough hot cocoa for the booth, more and more sold every day. She wasn't complaining; it just required figuring out exactly how to make enough for tomorrow after the ball tonight.

"Are you almost done here, Icelyn?" Holly asked as she cleaned up the bar area.

"I need to prepare the cocoa for tonight, Sleepy Time Hoot Cocoa, for after the masquerade."

"I can't believe you're sticking with that name. The one time you miswrite something in your notes, it inspires an entire nighttime brew of cocoa."

"I couldn't let genius like that go to waste. I just picture an owl getting ready for bed, but before turning in, he relaxes at the end of the night with a cocoa." Icelyn smiled, really happy with her ruby chocolate, chamomile, and warm spiced beverage. It was the most unique drink she had created, and she hoped it would be a hit tonight. "Can you get my dress and meet me at the palace? Maybe Douglas can take you and I'll take the shop cart."

"Who's handling the Sleepy Time tonight?"

"Envi said she would supervise the kitchen staff at the palace for me. She's been really helpful. I'm so glad Tasha introduced us. I don't think the festival would have been as successful without her help. Today especially." Icelyn's eyes welled with tears that she rapidly blinked back. Having friends, more friends than Holly, was a new experience for her.

"Sure, Douglas was already planning on taking both of us to the palace. Instead, I'll meet you there in an hour. Have someone point you to the dressing rooms. They are going to have a designated room for the ladies to rest and repair any clothing mishaps." Holly grabbed her bag. "See you soon." She skipped off with a little wave.

Icelyn's heart felt full. She sang as she brewed the chamomile tea and melted the ruby chocolate in creamy oat milk. As the chamomile tea steeped, she threw in a few cinnamon sticks, sprinkled some nutmeg and grated ginger into the milk. It wasn't long before everything was mixed, and she was wiping her hands on the apron covering her white top and black wool skirt. She loaded the cart, put on her matching wool coat and made her way to the palace.

Icelyn had never been on this road before, never having had a reason to visit the home of the king and queen. Her family had been invited in the past, but it was normally when her father was travelling and Maude never allowed her to do anything fun, much less go to an event where she might have taken attention away from Dru and Stacey.

It wasn't long before the buildings of town changed to the trees of the forest. Every detail of the drive became ingrained in her memory, including the traffic. As soon as the trees started to thin, she came to a row of carriages. Her shop cart did not fit in with the grand carriages, but she didn't have any other means of transportation to get to the castle. When she got there, a liveried servant directed her to the kitchen entrance, away from all the guests.

Icelyn quickly unloaded her cocoa with the help of Envi and a few of the castle's servants. She instructed them on how to heat everything up and serve it, even practiced the owl in the foam for the Hoot Cocoa. When she was confident Envi and the kitchen staff knew what they were doing, she headed to the stairs to find Holly, where she was stopped.

"You there, where do you think you are going?" the chef hollered.

Icelyn stopped and turned, looking around to see who this man was yelling at. She was the only person left in the area. "Are you yelling at me? Because I'm on the guest list for upstairs; I just have to go change."

"Sure, you are." The chef scoffed. "Not dressed like that you are. You should be in the kitchen with the rest of the temporary staff for the event."

"I just said I'm not going dressed like this. I'm here with the prince, I'm his date. And I was just about to go change into the gown that he bought for me." Icelyn turned to make her way upstairs to meet Holly, but it was no use. The chef grabbed her arm. "Excuse me, do not touch me." Indignant, Icelyn stared at him until he let go. That did not stop him from blocking her way up the stairs. There wasn't much she could do at this point. She was stuck, stuck working in the prince's kitchen when she should be upstairs skating next to him.

Icelyn wiped sweat from her brow after finishing the detailed decorations on the last of the appetizers for the masquerade. Somehow, she was spending her evening piping different savory sauces onto different delicious-looking foods when she should have been eating said food and enjoying the attention of a handsome prince. This was what she got for letting herself believe in the dream of one night off, one pretending she was a princess.

She sighed, and the sound reverberated around her. Glancing up, she noticed she was alone; now was her time to make a break for it, and hopefully find Holly and finish the night off in the way she dreamed. She took off the apron they had given her, checked her surroundings, and made a break for the stairs. Where she ran into what felt like a padded wall.

"Where do you think you're going? The night has just begun, I need you on desserts," Chef Henry said. "Don't even think about going above. I can't have you serving in that . . ." He looked her up and down, disapproval of her clothing in his eyes.

"I'm not going anywhere, just to the loo. I've been here for hours and need a moment," Icelyn said.

"Fine, but be quick. We have peppermint brownies and mini apple tarts still to prepare."

Icelyn rolled her eyes. His assumption that she was nothing more than staff for the event was getting old. She rubbed her temples and sighed. Unfortunately there was nothing she could do about it. She walked around the stout man, glancing back to see him watching her. It would seem making a break for it was not an option. The chef was a man who did not trust his staff, at least not the ones hired for just this event.

She pushed through the door to the servant's bathroom. There wasn't a mirror, but there was a bowl of water and a towel. She splashed some water on her face and dried it off, taking a deep breath as she did so. Shaking her arms, she jumped up and down a few times, and rolled her neck. Only the desserts to finish, and she would be able to make her way upstairs for the event. Find Holly, and hopefully be able to live her unrealistic dream for what was left of the night.

She walked back into the kitchen and Chef Henry was nowhere to be seen. However, the rest of the kitchen staff was there, and they all looked like lost puppies.

"Are there any instructions for what we are making tonight?" Icelyn asked the crowd in front of her.

"I couldn't find any. Chef Henry was called upstairs for some reason, and he left us here." The young woman tugged on her thick brown braid as she spoke.

"He mentioned peppermint brownies and mini apple tarts before I took my break. Do we have the ingredients for those?" Icelyn asked.

"I don't think so," the young woman answered. "We have some eggs, but I don't think we have enough for the brownies. Maybe half as many as we need."

"At least we have eggs. We just need to improvise." Icelyn looked at the ingredients.

There was chocolate, peppermint sugar, mint, and all the other essentials for baking, plus plenty of apples and cinnamon. She clapped her hands together. "We are going to make deep fried pastry sticks, cover it in peppermint sugar, and serve it with a peppermint sipping chocolate. The sipping chocolate is thicker than a hot cocoa, served hot in an espresso cup. We will need to let the guests know that you can both dip your fried pastry sticks in it, and drink it, whatever their preference is. Oh, and we have enough ingredients to make mini hand pies filled with a delicious apple and cinnamon filling."

She looked around at the rest of the staff. Everyone was nodding, if a bit wide-eyed still. But they looked eager to start. Icelyn gave instructions to each person, starting an assembly line for each of the desserts, while she handled the sipping chocolate. As annoyed as she was earlier, it all went away as the kitchen dance started. This was the best she had felt since she arrived at the palace. She was making things she loved, and it felt right.

She sent the last of the plates up to the rink with a couple of servers, wiped her hands on her apron, and sat down on the wooden bench in the corner of the kitchen. Every server who had come down the stairs had commented on how much everyone was talking about how delicious the desserts were. If she couldn't skate with the prince, serving her desserts was the next best thing. It actually might even be better than skating with the prince.

"Oh my gods, you saved us. Everyone loved what you made," the young sous chef said.

"It was a team effort." She gave the young woman a hug. Her support and talent had been essential to the evening's success.

"Now go, see if the prince is waiting for you."

Chapter Twenty

Colden drummed his fingers on the arm of his throne, the one that sat in between his father and brother, overseeing the entire event. His eyes passed over the throne his sister had never sat in and the one his mother used to occupy, ignoring the pain caused from missing them. He was *at* the event, not *part* of it. He couldn't wait to go down to the ice and skate with Icelyn, but she wasn't there yet. His eyes scanned the crowd again. No one who even resembled her was there. He didn't see her unique colorful hair that made her stand out in a crowd. The dress he sent her was nowhere to be seen. He shifted in his seat as he looked over the crowd again. There were two redheads skating together. If Holly and Douglas were here, where was Icelyn? He shifted again as his gaze darted across the ice one more time.

"Who are you looking for, son?" the king asked.

Colden's head whipped over to look at his father. "What? I mean, why would you think I'm looking for anyone?"

"It's fairly obvious. The constant shifting in your seat, the impatient sighs. Eyes looking over the crowd, over and over again. Seems to me you've found someone and are meeting with them tonight. Does this mean you've made a decision?"

"I don't have an answer for that yet. But I was supposed to meet someone here. We've been spending time together during the festival." Colden swiped his hand through his hair, uncomfortable with the conversation. He wasn't used to sharing things with his father, especially things like this.

"According to town gossip, the two of you have been spending a lot of time together—some of it alone, in the ice maze." Ollie elbowed him. Leave it to a younger brother to turn his life into a joke.

"I hope you decide soon, and I get to meet this person. Anyone that has you this fidgety must be worth meeting," the king said.

The band stopped playing with a screech and silence fell over the room. The three of them followed the gaze of everyone in the room, across the ice, towards the entrance. In the doorway was Icelyn, or so he assumed. A masked petite woman stood in the dress he had sent. Her hair tumbled down in waves of pinks, blues, purples, and silvers, matching the tones of the dress as the light hit it.

Colden let out the breath he was holding. She was here; relief flooded through him. He thought she had stood him up, skipped the event altogether. But there she was, looking almost exactly as he imagined her when he bought the dress and the skates. The dress didn't fit quite as he had imagined, but she was still a vision.

He stood as the masked woman made her way through the crowd to the dais. She seemed to be struggling to cross the ice, clutching the wall to keep her balance. The minute he saw the dress in the shop, he knew she would look like a queen in it, and she did not disappoint. Even if she wasn't as graceful on the ice as he assumed she would be. But it seemed she loved something she wasn't actually good at, and who could fault her for that? Out of the corner of his eye, he saw Holly and Douglas waving frantically, but he was enraptured by Icelyn. The two of them continued to wave, trying to get his attention. He ignored them, more concerned with meeting up with the woman coming towards him ever so slowly, lacking any of the natural grace he thought Icelyn would have from all their other conversations.

They met at the edge of the ice, right where the ice and the sitting area met. Colden looked back at his father to see him nod his approval. The prince grinned, stepped onto the ice, and took his date into his arms without saying a word.

The skating was slow, nothing like he'd imagined when he purchased the dress. He had pictured gliding over the ice, two as one, waltzing to the notes of the lute as they drifted through the crowd. However, his date lacked the skill and grace to do that: she clung to him as her feet went this way and that, unable to control their direction, almost tumbling to the ground multiple times. It was all he could do to hold her up and not crash to the ice himself as she lost control yet again.

Through gritted teeth he asked, "Would you like to take a seat over at the café? I believe dessert is being served now."

His date nodded in assent but did not utter a single word.

Strange, Colden thought. Icelyn was never silent; she always had something to say to him, something she wanted him to think about. He shook his head, as if doing so would get rid of his wayward thoughts. Maybe she was overwhelmed by the event and that's why she was silent.

Douglas and Holly skated into his view. He raised his hand to call them over, but his date stopped him mid-motion, then gestured to a table for two. Instead of having their friends join them, he escorted her to the private table, pulled out her chair, and then sat himself, unsure of how sitting together would go since she still hadn't said anything the entire night.

"How was your day?" the prince asked.

His date just shrugged as the waiter stopped at the table and put two plates of something before them. It was not part of the menu he had designed for the night, but it looked delicious, some type of fried pastry stick with a sipping chocolate. Before trying it himself, he watched his date take a dainty bite of the chocolate-covered dough. He saw her eyes widen with surprise, but it quickly turned to what looked like panic as her eyes darted around the room. She sighed in relief, or so it seemed, as her eyes focused back on him.

"You look lovely in the dress," Colden said.

His date blushed prettily. She looked away with a slight giggle. Was he supposed to think that was a thank you? It was so out of character for her to not acknowledge the compliment. It was even unusual for her to blush.

"Prince Colden, I need to talk to you. It's urgent," Douglas interrupted.

"I'm sure it can wait." Colden blew off his friend.

"Actually, Your Highness, it cannot," Douglas whispered.

"Is there an emergency of state I have to deal with?"

"No, it's just that . . .," Douglas started.

"Then, as you can see, I'm busy." Colden pushed Douglas away and turned back to his date.

He grabbed a piece of the fried pastry stick and dipped it into the chocolate. She snatched it out of his hand and set it on the plate. She stood and grabbed his arm, dragging him back to the ice.

"I have to go find her. Whoever that is in her dress, it's definitely not Icelyn," Colden heard as he passed by Holly and Douglas. He tried to stop to hear more, but his date and the crowd pushed him towards the ice. He looked back to see Holly walk away from Douglas. Maybe he should have given his friend a chance to speak. He looked back at his silent date and noticed that she seemed taller than Icelyn and her hair didn't shimmer in the light the same way. It was like everything was just a tiny bit off. He was about to take off the woman's mask when she stumbled on the ice, pulling him down with her.

He took great care to stand up. Offering a hand to his date, he helped her back onto her skates. He slipped his arm around what felt like her heavily corseted waist before helping her off the ice once again.

"Maybe we should stay off the ice for the rest of the night; I think it will be safer for the both of us." Colden held her up as he carefully skated to the edge of the ice where there were more tables. He sat his date down and purposefully made eye contact with a server, using the eye contact to request a dessert for the two of them. This time he intended to get a bite of it.

The server brought the fried pastry stick and sipping chocolate out to them, carefully setting it in the middle of the table. He snagged a piece and a small cup of the chocolate. After dipping the fried dough into the chocolate, he took a bite. His date half stood, like she wanted to stop him. But it was too late, the crispy, fluffy dough seemed to melt in his mouth under the rich minty chocolate. It was there again, that feeling he had when he took a sip of the peppermint hot cocoa a couple of weeks ago. It felt like happiness, love, and a hug wrapped together. He had to meet the person who made this. It was like the person knew his heart somehow, and he knew they knew because of how their creations made him feel. He took another bite, forgetting about his date, the one that had felt wrong all night long.

He stood. The need to find whoever had made the chocolate dessert was more important than anything else. His date stood moments after him. He watched as she took a step towards him, tripping over the chair and falling right into his arms. A blonde curl slipped out from under the silvery and pastel hair.

"You've got to be kidding me!"

Colden looked up to see Icelyn staring at him with a woman wearing her dress in his arms. The look of betrayal on her face nearly brought him to his knees.

He watched as the woman he thought he was spending the evening with stood by herself, dressed in a plain black skirt and white shirt covered in flour, while he held an imposter in his arms. He set whoever was in his arms aside and took a step towards Icelyn.

She held up her hand. "Don't. I can't right now. I just can't." She turned and ran out of the building.

For a moment he just stood there, stunned. But only for a moment. Once the moment sunk in, he went after her. However, he was unable to find her as hordes of people seemed to close in behind her, allowing her to disappear into the night.

Chapter Twenty-One

"Oh my gods, Icelyn, where have you been? I've looked for you everywhere." Holly gasped, finding Icelyn in the servants' stairwell.

"Apparently you didn't look in the kitchen." Icelyn shrugged.

"Why would you be in the kitchen? You're supposed to be on the ice floating around like a magic princess, not cooking."

"True, instead I was co-opted by the chef, who disappeared right before dessert. He didn't believe me when I said I was a guest, and I never got the chance to look for you and my dress. That man ruined my night off by insisting I was here to work. And I'm not even going to get paid for it, because I wasn't supposed to be working." Icelyn continued up the stairs. She was determined to enjoy some of the masquerade tonight.

"That's why I've been looking for you. Your dress, the skates, they weren't there. Everything was gone." Holly looked like she wanted to cry.

"Again? Why is this happening to me?" She almost sat on the stairs in despair. Instead, she quickened her step, taking two stairs at a time.

"It's worse." Holly gasped for breath. "Someone is here wearing your dress, hanging out with the prince for most of the evening. Actually, she's been hanging on him."

Icelyn burst through the door that led to the masquerade. As soon as she crossed the threshold, she came to a screeching halt, which caused Holly to slam into her.

"You've got to be kidding me!" Icelyn exclaimed.

She couldn't believe it; the prince was standing there with a woman wearing the dress he gave Icelyn in his arms. The woman was even wearing a wig to mimic her hair. At the sound of her voice, both Colden and the woman turned to look at her standing there, mouth agape, covered in flour, hair tied back atop her head. Basically, she looked like a hot mess surrounded by hundreds of elegantly dressed people.

Her cheeks felt warm, and her palms were sweating. She could hear her heart pounding as she stood there, the center of attention. She couldn't stand here with everyone staring at her another moment. Especially in front of the prince who was holding someone else in his arms. The woman turned her head slightly and a gold curl slipped through the pastel strands. The prince set the fraud aside and started towards Icelyn.

She held up her hand. "Don't. I can't right now. I just can't." She turned and ran out of the building. The fall of her footsteps echoed around her as she ran from the Ice Masquerade Ball and through the halls of the palace. She heard both Holly and Colden call for her to stop, but she couldn't stop. She needed to be home, away from all of this. The break-ins, the sabotage, the stolen items, and now her stolen night. It was too much, and it had all started when she met the prince. As much as she liked him, she wasn't sure if it was worth it, if he was worth it. Especially if he didn't even recognize that she wasn't who had been with him this evening, just someone dressed like her.

"Icelyn, are you okay?" Holly asked, panting from the run.

Icelyn turned. "You didn't have to follow me. I can find my way home." She turned back to the road, the snow crunching under her feet with each and every step. She could hear Holly's steps in between hers.

"I'm not here to make sure you get home . . . Okay, that's part of why I'm here. I wasn't going to let you walk through the woods alone. We're friends: this is what friends do for each other."

"Fine, but I don't want to talk about any of this." Icelyn shoved her hands into her pockets.

"We don't have to talk about anything at all." Holly waited . . . one moment . . . then another.

"It's just that he didn't even recognize that it wasn't me. Am I that blasé that as long as someone looks like the right person, it's fine?" Icelyn walked briskly, her anger fueling her.

"I don't think that's exactly what happened. I think he got caught up in the moment, worried you weren't going to show, and then this woman appeared in the dress he bought you." Holly panted, trying to keep up with her friend.

"Are you making excuses for him? I spent all evening making the food for the ball instead of being at the ball. And don't get me wrong, I enjoyed it, especially when the chef disappeared. He left the kitchen short on ingredients, so I actually had the chance to create something of my own. But it wasn't right that Colden was with someone else the entire time. He didn't even realize it wasn't me." Her arms flailed wildly as she ranted about the prince. She couldn't help herself. Prior to this she thought she was falling for him. But now she wasn't sure.

"Maybe . . ."

Icelyn stopped walking. "There's no maybe. On top of tonight, ever since I met the prince so many things have gone wrong. I want them to stop, and they will if I stop seeing him. That's what I have to do. I have to stop seeing him. It's that simple." Icelyn nodded her head like she had just made the best decision she would ever make in her life. She turned back to the path to continue her walk home.

"Are you sure? He's done a lot to help you out. The contract for the festival, all of Douglas's help. I wouldn't want you to lose any of that if you break it off with him right now." Holly chewed her lip; concern etched her face.

"I don't think he's that petty. Besides, we have regulars now. Even if we weren't providing hot cocoa at all the events, we would still have customers. I don't think they are going to disappear. Think about it. We have Henry,

Danny, Francine, and so many others that come by every day. I can make it without the prince." Her pace sped up, determination fueling her. She had planning to do that for the rest of the festival. "You know what, I think I'm going to enter the hot cocoa competition. It's a blind taste testing so it won't matter who the judges are. I can win."

"I can't argue with that, and I've been trying to convince you to enter the contest for—oh I don't know, forever." Holly crossed her arms. "Aren't you cold?"

"No, it's a beautiful night, and I'm not going to let tonight get me down or keep me down. Oh no, I left my cart at the castle." She stopped mid-step and looked back at the castle. Her entire body sagged in defeat.

"I'm sure Douglas can bring it down tomorrow. I'll send a message when we get to your shop. It's an easy fix," Holly said.

"Thank you, you're a life saver." She stopped to give her best friend a hug.

Snow fell as the two of them walked the rest of the way in silence. By the time they were at her cottage, it was really coming down. There was enough snow to make her worry about the outdoor booth tomorrow. If enough snow fell it would be difficult, if not impossible, to get supplies over to the events.

"The snow is really coming down." Holly echoed what she had been thinking.

"I know, I'm worried about tomorrow. What if we can't get supplies to the booth for the events?" Icelyn chewed on her thumbnail.

"There's nothing we can do about the snow, so it's not worth worrying about. Now unlock the door so we can warm up by the fire. I'm freezing." Holly jumped up and down.

"It's not that bad." Icelyn took her keys out and unlocked the door. The door swung open, and waiting right inside was Ember, flapping her wings in excitement.

"Hi, sweetie, did you have a good night?" She bent over to pick up her pet dragon. "I missed you tonight. Thank you for not burning the place down."

"Why are you two so cute? I can't handle it."

Icelyn pointed to the fireplace. "Ember, can you light the fire for us?"

Ember flapped her wings in front of Icelyn and gave a little poof of smoke in her excitement. She flew over to the fireplace and blew until the fire was lit and warming the room.

"Good girl, Ember, such a good job." Icelyn patted her on the head.

Holly plopped down on to the yellow sofa by the fireplace.

"Do you want me to tell Douglas to stop coming by?" Holly asked with hesitation.

"Why would I want that? He's a friend and your beau. I would never ask you to keep someone you like away from the café." Icelyn joined her friend on the sofa. "Colden and I weren't meant to make it. It started out as fake, and turns out it never changed for him. I'm just thankful I didn't let myself fall too hard." She drifted off as she watched the dancing flames in the fireplace. She felt Ember lay down with her, snuggled behind her knees, and didn't even stir when her friend laid a blanket over her and wished her goodnight.

Chapter Twenty-Two

Forgetting about the woman he had spent the evening with, Colden went after Icelyn. Until Douglas stepped in front of him. Colden pushed him to the side, but the great wall of a man was immovable.

"Give her a moment," Douglas murmured. "She's going to need time after tonight."

"I need to explain to her what happened. She needs to know I didn't mean for the night to go this way." Colden pushed Douglas aside, or at least attempted to do so.

"That may be what you need right now, but what she needs is more important. At least, it should be, if you care for her."

"Fine, but I don't like it. I don't like it at all." Colden sat at the table. He picked up the cup of chocolate and took a sip. As frustrated as he was, an overwhelming sense of happiness came over him. He almost felt like singing, or maybe dancing. "Who made this? Who was in charge of dessert tonight? Where is Chef Henry?"

Colden looked around the room; only a few servers remained. Each of those servers was looking at him. He cleared his throat. One of the young servers stepped forward, carrying a tray of the fried pastry sticks and sipping chocolate.

"Your Highness, Chef Henry disappeared before dessert this evening. He was called up here to answer questions and never returned."

"Thank you, Miss . . . ?"

"Amalie, sir."

"Thank you, Amalie. Who made the dessert? It wasn't on the menu for tonight."

"I don't know what her name is, but Chef Henry kept this woman in the kitchen, even though she said she was supposed to be attending the masquerade. It's a good thing she was in the kitchen with us though. We would have been lost without her. When Chef left, I discovered we were short on ingredients. This woman came up with the idea for the desserts tonight. When she was done, it was like she just disappeared."

"Did you get her name? Wait, you just said you didn't know what her name was. Did you find out anything about her? Anything that will help me find her?" Colden begged.

"I'm sorry, she was dressed like a server. And we were busy all night long. Running things up and down the stairs. And there were a lot of extra staff for tonight." Amalie's eyes darted around the crowd. The tray shook in her hands.

Colden watched as the server's nerves became apparent. He took a deep breath, making the woman who had talked to him nervous was not his goal. "I'm sorry, why don't you set your tray down. I'm sure it gets heavy after a while." Colden took the tray from her, setting it down on one of the tables behind him. "Thank you for your help." He clasped her hand in thanks.

"What do you want to do now, Your Highness?" Douglas asked.

"The masquerade should continue on. Maestro, music please." Colden gestured to have everything start again. He nodded his head to a hall, indicating that Douglas should follow him.

The crowd moved out of his way as he made his way to a private area. His gaze swept over the crowd looking for the woman who wore the dress he purchased for Icelyn. The woman he had spent the evening with. The woman who had him not trusting himself . . . because he had thought things were off, but she was wearing the dress he purchased for Icelyn. He never thought someone else would be wearing it tonight. But that's what happened, and now he felt like he was on the verge of losing someone he liked having in his life because of it.

Then there was this other person, the person who made delicious, magical chocolate beverages. Drinks that made him feel happiness and love. Drinks that somehow made him feel understood, that made him want to sing and dance. He needed to meet this person, he felt connected to them. But how could he mend things with Icelyn and chase whoever made the dessert tonight, and why did he have this overwhelming need to do both?

"The hot cocoa person was here tonight," Colden said, stopping in the private hall and turning towards Douglas.

"You mean Icelyn; yes, she was here tonight, and she's angry because she saw you spending time with someone who wasn't her, and you didn't realize it wasn't her." Douglas crossed his arms.

"Icelyn was here, but that's not who I'm talking about. I'm talking about magic cocoa. The cocoa that made me fall in love with whoever made it. That person was here tonight. They were in the kitchen; they made the dessert."

"Oh my gods . . .," Douglas exclaimed before muttering something Colden could not hear.

"What did you say?"

"Nothing, Your Highness. I'm curious as to why you are so interested in this person you've never met? Especially when you seem to care so much about Icelyn. You went searching for Ember for her. And you went shopping . . . shopping! It's clear that you like her. Why would you even risk causing more damage to your relationship after tonight?" Douglas leaned against the wall.

"I can't explain it. There's something about the cocoa or tonight's sipping chocolate that makes me feel like I'm at home. I can't ignore it. I'm not sure I could if I wanted to. But I don't want to, I want to know who makes these delicious things. These things cause me to feel like I've never felt before. Why should I ignore that?" Colden ran his hand through his hair, pacing as he felt the pressure to make a decision he wasn't ready to make.

"Maybe because you've been feeling a similar connection to a person you've met and spent time with. Why would you throw that away for a feeling you get based on drinking something? I've had those drinks too, and you're right. They make me feel good too. But you know what makes me feel even better? Spending time with Holly. I wouldn't trade that in for something as intangible as a feeling I get from a drink." Douglas looked like he wanted to shake some sense into Colden but didn't want to risk losing his job. Instead, he stood there, arms crossed, casually leaning up against the wall. All while Colden paced up and down the hall.

"I'm not you, Douglas, I don't know how to give up on something without having figured out who is behind the drinks and what makes them so magical. I need answers, but how am I going to get them?" Colden stroked his chin as he thought. "I know." He snapped. "You're not going to like this, Douglas. But I have a plan." With those final words he took off to the dais, and his father.

Before Douglas could stop him, Colden was in front of his father. He gestured to the musicians to stop playing.

"What is the meaning of this? What is going on, son?" the king asked his eldest son.

"I have an announcement to make," Colden stated with a confidence he wasn't actually feeling.

"Now, right before the unmasking of tonight's masquerade?"

"Yes, now. You see, Father, I've taken your words to heart. You want me engaged by the end of the Snow Solstice Festival. Well, I have decided how I am going to choose my partner." Colden crossed his arms and squared his shoulders.

"Well then, spit it out, boy. How are you choosing your partner?"

"In four days, it will be the last day of the festival, and the final event will be the hot cocoa competition. The winner of the event will become my consort. I will judge the competition myself. That way the winner will be the one who makes the cocoa I tasted a week ago and again tonight."

A murmur swept through the crowd. Indicating most could not believe what they were hearing. This would be an opportunity for anyone to become the next consort to the king, the next ruler of Wynterfell.

"Son, you cannot choose your partner in life based on hot cocoa. What are you thinking?"

"What am I thinking? You're the one who gave me this ridiculous ultimatum. I've tasted things this week that make me feel like the person who made it knows me better than anyone else. And they've never met me in person. So, this is my response to your ultimatum." Colden waived at the crowd as he spoke to his father through a pasted-on smile. "Everyone gets what they want in the end, right? That was your goal." With that, Colden nodded one last time to the crowd and walked off the dais.

He heard the sputtering of his father and the footsteps of his lumbering friend behind him. But they didn't stop Colden from going directly to his chambers.

Chapter Twenty-Three

Icelyn woke up with Ember snuggled up next to her. It took her a moment to realize where she was, as it was not her tiny bedroom next door to the café. It would seem that she had fallen asleep while talking to Holly last night, and Holly had left her on the cushy yellow sofa by the fireplace when she locked up. Icelyn couldn't blame her. As much as she would like to say her bedroom was nice, it wasn't, yet. It was functional, but that's all it had going for it.

"I was just about to wake you. To help out, I started some of the baked goods for the booth, but I couldn't find a recipe for a specialty hot cocoa for today. I wasn't sure you had decided what you were serving since, well, you know." Holly walked in wiping her hands on a towel.

"Oh gods! What time is it? I have to put something together quickly. Do I even have time to create something for today?" Icelyn pushed herself off the sofa, stumbling to her feet. Good thing her friend was there: she might have gone crashing to the floor if Holly hadn't steadied her.

"Icelyn, I woke you up with plenty of time. It's only three a.m. You have at least two hours to get everything ready, if not longer. I've already packed up all the basic ingredients and the large-size pots to take to the booth. You just need to decide on the specialty cocoa for today," Holly said, grabbing Icelyn by the shoulders to ensure she listened.

"You're a lifesaver. If you don't mind, can you go next door and grab the cash box? My mother's recipe book is in there. I need to get ready for the day before I can start thinking of what to make. I will meet you there when I'm done." Icelyn ran upstairs, barely hearing her friend's response to her question. "Ember, can you warm up the water for me?" Icelyn pointed to the jug of water sitting on the washstand.

Ember flapped her wings, carefully landing by the jug. Icelyn saw her blow a small, controlled breath of fire before she threw off her clothes from the night before. She grabbed a towel and her favorite winter citrus soap and wiped yesterday off her with the help of the steaming water and her soap. Grabbing a clean chemise, she threw it on over her head before brushing her teeth and fixing her hair. She looked through her clothing. She needed to feel pretty today, so she decided on her favorite gown, an icy-blue wool dress (that in no way reminded her of Colden's eyes) under a dove grey wool coat with matching blue trim. The sleeves of the coat laced up over the long sleeves of the dress, helping to keep both out of the way while she cooked all day. After Chef Henry dismissed her because of her clothing yesterday evening, she refused to dress in anything plain. And this outfit, a gift from her father, with the short capelet and hood on the coat, the matching trim, and the soft quality of the wool, always made her feel like a queen. Even if no one had ever seen her in it because she was in the back kitchen at Maude's.

She walked outside and into her café, and Holly whistled as she entered, causing her to smile.

"Aren't you looking elegant today?" Holly said, her appreciation for the outfit clear in her eyes.

"Thank you, after being mistaken for a servant yesterday, I needed a little something extra today." Icelyn twirled as she hit the bottom of the stairs.

"It looks stunning, I hope it's not going to get in the way of making the cocoa." Holly held out a leather-bound notebook. "Is this your mother's recipe book?"

Icelyn grabbed the book and hugged it before setting it down on the counter. She paged through the book, caressing certain pages, like the peppermint hot cocoa recipe—her and her mother's favorite. She remembered working with her mom in a messy kitchen, helping to mix all the ingredients together. Her mom had to hold her up so she was tall enough to stir things on the stove. The memories of messy kitchens and sipping hot cocoa by the roaring fire were some of her favorites. It was a time when they were all happy together . . . before things changed.

She shook her head. She couldn't do peppermint again; she had made something similar last night, and she wanted to enter that recipe into the contest. The question was—did she want something that brought about cozy vibes with every sip, or something that mimicked the crisp, cold weather? There were two recipes in the notebook that stood out to her, a peanut butter hot cocoa and an orange cardamon hot cocoa. The first reminded her of curling up with a good book, but the second reminded her of waking up on a winter morning to go snow shoeing, packing hot cocoa and oranges for snacks along the way. Her mouth salivated at the thought, especially when she remembered the cardamom buns. She should make those too. They would be such a hit at the festival.

"Holly, I'm thinking orange cardamon hot cocoa and cardamom buns. We have just enough time to make them if we hurry. Can you start on the buns? I'll get the orange zest and cardamon steeping in the milk." Icelyn felt her excitement bubble over as she gathered the ingredients. It wasn't long before she was humming and dancing while she worked.

She looked over to see Holly rolling out the dough, spreading the cardamom filling, folding the dough over, slicing the dough, then making the buns, before setting them aside to rise for a second time. Holly did all this while Icelyn worked on the base of today's hot cocoa concoction. She had every burner on her stove filled with pots of oat milk with orange zest and cardamon, so she hopefully had enough base before adding the cocoa at the booth. While her orange concoction came to life, she sliced oranges to decorate the mugs and put them on the plates next to the cardamom buns. The initial rush turned into a fantastic morning as she worked with her best friend. When they finished, they loaded up her shop cart and made their way to the festival booth. Icelyn wasn't sure who had brought it back for her, but she was thankful.

Today, the festival was all about shopping for Solstice gifts. There were only four days left until the end of the Snow Solstice Festival. Today was dedicated to helping all the businesses in town and the artisans at the marketplace, tomorrow was the snowball battle, the next day was another market day, and the festival ended with the hot cocoa competition and bonfire. She planned to step away for a bit today to do some shopping. She wanted to get Holly and Douglas something. They had been indispensable to her success during the festival. She hoped Envi remembered to show up to help out so she could escape for a little while.

"We're here," Holly said as they arrived at the booth.

"My mind is here, there, and everywhere today. It barely took any time to get here this morning," Icelyn responded.

They quickly unpacked the cart. Icelyn had just grabbed the last of the orange, spiced oat milk when Dru and Stacey came up to her.

"Good morning, Icelyn. Funny running into you here." Dru's smile looked more like a sneer as he greeted her.

"What do you two want?" Icelyn sighed.

"We were just wondering if you were planning on entering the hot cocoa contest?" Stacey giggled.

"As of right now, I'm not sure I'll have time. Business is actually keeping me quite busy at the moment."

"That's too bad, I guess we will just have to win it again," Dru gloated. The twins walked by Icelyn, causing her to drop her orange mixture, spilling it all over the outfit she had so carefully picked out, while not a single drop landed on Dru or Stacey.

"Oh my gods, Icelyn, what happened?" Holly asked as Icelyn walked into the booth.

"Dru and Stacey happened. They are the absolute worst. I can't continue to live like this. I don't know if it's my interactions with the prince or the fact that my booth is successful . . . or both. But they are out to get me, and it's putting a damper on everything good that's happening." Icelyn grabbed a towel and tried to clean herself up. But it was no use. She would be lucky if her wool coat wasn't completely ruined.

"Go get changed before you freeze. I'll start another batch of the orange cardamon milk while you change. It won't be as good as yours because it's lacking in magic, but at least there will be backup when everyone decides . . . What are you calling the orange cardamon cocoa?"

"I don't know. It reminds me of snow shoeing with my parents, so I was thinking something like Snowy Adventures."

"I love it, I'll write up the board while you're gone too. Don't let Dru and Stacey ruin your day. Remember, what goes around comes around, and they will eventually get what's coming to them."

"I sure hope so. I can't handle much more of this." Icelyn pointed down at her dress before heading back to her house.

The ride back was short; the only bad moment was when she passed Mother Maude's and the entire family decided to come outside to point at her and talk, like they weren't the cause of her current predicament. She tried to take the high road and ignore them, which was becoming more difficult by the day. She wanted to scream and rail at them. But if her past experiences had taught her anything, it was that it wouldn't matter what she did; they would continue causing mischief and nothing would happen to them.

She unlocked the door and ran to her bedroom. She quickly changed into her second favorite wool dress and coat. It was just like the other one in design, but the colors were black and pink instead of grey and blue. It looked pretty with her hair, but she always liked the blue one better. She took a deep breath in an effort to reset her mood. She felt like she looked nice once again, she was happy with her creations, and there was nothing to spill on her this time. She let out the breath, along with the tension, she was holding on to.

She made her way back to the booth, sure she would succeed in getting there without incident. That was, until she saw the prince standing on the road in front of her. As much as she wanted to avoid this conversation, it looked like it was going to happen, whether she was ready or not.

Chapter Twenty-Four

"Icelyn, wait! Can we talk?" Colden called after her.

She stopped her horse and cart in front of him. "I would prefer not. I have a busy day ahead."

Colden looked baffled by her answer, like he was unsure what to do as he struggled to respect her wishes all while feeling the desperate need to explain himself and have her forgive him.

Icelyn watched as a myriad of emotions ran across his face. She was tempted to continue on her way, but she also knew she needed to tell him that she had to end their . . . whatever it was they had together because it was ruining her life. Or at least it felt like it was ruining her life. Maybe it was something else, but nothing this bad had happened to her until they started spending time together. Sure, the twins caused her problems, but the amount of destruction now was worse than anything they'd done before.

"Fine, we can talk now. But we have to hurry. I need to get to my booth. My backup doesn't show up until later today, and I don't want Holly there alone for the morning rush. The morning has already been trying enough." Icelyn got out of the cart so she could walk with the prince. She saw Dru and Stacey watching her as she did so. Did those two have nothing better to do than follow her around town? Rolling her eyes at their antics, she turned to the prince. "What do you want to talk about?"

"Last night. I knew there was something off about the woman I was with. But I couldn't figure out how anyone would have gotten their hands on the dress I gave you. So . . ." Colden trailed off.

"You couldn't figure it out? Since I met you, my shop has been broken into multiple times, ingredients stolen, furniture destroyed. It's so bad I can't even open it right now. Which I've made work because I have a booth at the festival. Is it really so shocking that someone would break in and steal the dress?" Icelyn's hands made their way to her hips in indignation.

"But why would no one tell me? I thought you had stood me up. But then someone was there, with your hair and in the dress. What should I have thought?"

Icelyn sighed. "I don't know what you should have thought. I wasn't the one waiting. I was the one who went to the castle, where I was kept as a servant because I didn't dress nicely enough, and then saved the day when the chef disappeared. I tried to get to the masquerade multiple times throughout the night, but was prevented from it. And it's not like anyone came looking for me."

"That's not true. Holly and Douglas looked for you . . . Come to think of it, I think Douglas tried to warn me, but I didn't listen to him."

"You are not helping your case, Your Highness. Why wouldn't you listen to your best friend? If you had, maybe you could have done something to make the night go better. Instead, I felt rejected at every turn." Icelyn sniffed. She could feel the tears welling up. Rejection was something she was used to, and last night had brought all those feelings back. The events of this morning didn't help.

Colden stared at her. He looked unsure of himself, of how to make things right, especially since he was admitting he was wrong. A place he seemed unfamiliar with. "I'm sorry. If I could do it all over again, I would. But since I can't, what can I do to make it better?"

"For now, I need you to leave me alone. I need to finish out the festival and rebuild my shop. I don't have time for our fake relationship. It's just that . . . I also don't know if . . . never mind. I need to go work." Before he could say anything, Icelyn climbed into the cart and drove off, leaving him standing there, alone and confused.

He didn't know how long he stood there staring in the direction Icelyn had gone. It could have been minutes or hours. He felt like he was missing something from the conversation. Something about where she had spent the evening. It felt like he had heard it before, but where?

"Prince Colden, whatever are you doing standing in the cold all by your lonesome?" Dru sauntered up to him, distracting the prince from his musings.

Colden turned to walk away like he hadn't heard anything and almost ran over Stacey. Dammit, he was trapped.

"Is it true you're going to marry whoever wins the hot cocoa competition?" Stacey asked.

"That is what I announced last night." He needed to escape these two. He looked around and saw Tasha. "Ah, I have to go. I have an important interview. Tasha!" He waved to her.

Tasha stopped mid-step. It was rare, beyond rare, for the prince to say anything to the press. "Yes, Your Highness, are you ready for our interview?"

"Yes, Tasha, I am. Why don't we find a quiet place to talk?" He turned to Dru and Stacey. "I'm sorry, I must be going. Have a nice day."

"He's insufferable. It's like no one has ever told him no in his life. He is a prince, so maybe no one has ever told him no. I just can't deal with him right now." Icelyn jumped down from the cart, tying the reins to a post before turning towards Holly. Holly was not alone; Douglas was in the booth as well. Not surprising, but it did limit her ability to complain about the prince.

"I take it you ran into the prince today?" Douglas asked. "Don't let me stop you. He is all the things you are thinking and probably more. And he hasn't been presenting himself in a positive light recently. The announcement about the hot cocoa competition is a perfect example of that."

"What are you talking about?" Holly turned towards Douglas, her eyebrow raised.

"He thinks he's in love with the person who made the sipping chocolate last night and the peppermint hot cocoa from when we first met. So, he's decided to marry whoever he determines is the winner of the hot cocoa contest." Douglas rolled his eyes.

"But I made both of those things. Does he not know what I do?" Icelyn crossed her arms.

"He hasn't made the connection. He can be a bit dense at times," Douglas said.

" 'A bit dense?' " Icelyn's voice raised an octave. "This is more than 'a bit dense.' He's straight up clueless. No wonder he didn't know it wasn't me last night. He hasn't paid attention to anything that's happened while we were together. He's a fool. And I'm a fool for thinking I liked him. And you, why haven't you told him?" She jabbed Douglas in the chest.

Douglas opened his mouth, then shut it, His cheeks turned so red they matched his hair.

"Icelyn, you are not a fool. Prince Colden, maybe. But he also has a lot going on. His father . . .," Holly started.

"Why are you making excuses for him? He doesn't deserve them." Icelyn glared at Holly.

"He may not, but you do. You like him, and he's done things to help you that no one else ever has. I just think he deserves to be heard—when you are ready."

"Whatever, customers will be here any minute. I need to get ready." Icelyn pushed her way to the stove. She wasn't in the mood to give the prince a chance. Or to hear how hard things were for him, even if it was true. She wanted to wallow, at least for a little bit. But she heard someone clear their voice. She looked up to see the line had formed in mere moments, and as always, Danny was in the front of the line. "Good morning, Danny. What can I get you this morning?"

"You know I have to try your special of the day. A Snowy Adventure with a cardamom bun. I don't know if I've ever had a pastry from you that doesn't have chocolate. This is a treat."

"Thanks, Danny, I do love chocolate, but I can do other things." She handed him his order. "Hi,

Amalie, I'm surprised to see you out this early after last night."

"I heard this booth was yours, and I had to try it after watching you in the kitchen last night. Plus, the prince's announcement. If he knew it was you, I bet he would propose," Amalie said.

"Ugh, don't remind me. I don't know how he doesn't know it was me. He's clueless."

"Are you going to enter the competition?" Amalie took the pastry from Icelyn.

"Me? No, I don't think so. He should already know it's me. Clueless man. But thank you for stopping by today. It's nice to see you again." Icelyn stepped from behind the booth to give the young woman a hug.

The day went on like that, new customers from the castle's kitchen asking her about entering into the competition. Her regulars kept telling her about the announcement, begging her to enter. She was about to shut the booth down for the day because she was tired of hearing about it when Tasha and Envi showed up.

"Thank gods you're here. Please take over. I can't do this anymore. I need to step away before I actually scream." Icelyn took off her apron and handed it to Envi.

Tasha looked at Icelyn. "I was going to ask if we could talk, but I'm not sure if you're in the best mood for an interview."

"I may not be, but come shopping with me. Maybe a little retail therapy will have me feeling better. And you can get your article. I know I promised to keep you up to date on what is happening with the prince. I'll keep my promise."

"For now, let's just walk around and shop. No pressure for anything more. If you decide you want to share, you can, but if not, there's always tomorrow." Tasha took Icelyn by the arm, and they headed to the marketplace.

"I don't understand why you're being so nice to me. I've always thought of the press as ruthless. But you've been kind and supportive ever since we met." She looked over at the reporter who was feeling more and more like a friend every day.

"I don't think you have to be cutthroat to get a good story every single time. Sometimes it's necessary, but most of the time, people want to be heard. I help people fulfill that need. So, if you want Wynterfell to hear you, I can help make that happen. If you prefer to stay invisible, it's impossible to be heard."

"I don't know, Tasha; I've always been in the background. No one ever saw me or heard me. Why should things change now? Why should it change since the prince has tasted the things that I make, and he wants to marry the person who makes them? But he doesn't know that the person making them is me?" Icelyn heard a gasp; she turned towards the noise to see blonde curls bounce as a woman ran off. "I'm screwed, I'm pretty sure that was Stacey and she heard everything."

Chapter Twenty-Five

"I don't know what to do, Douglas. Icelyn won't talk to me; she wants to call off the entire thing. But I don't feel right about it just ending. I really like spending time with her." Colden paced in his room. His frantic movement slowed to a stop in front of the stone fireplace. The fire roared in between the stone walls of the fireplace, radiating heat into the cold room. One of the two wingback chairs was occupied by Douglas, who watched Colden struggle with his recent decisions, especially his more impulsive ones.

"Should have thought of that before spending the evening with someone who wasn't Icelyn. Why didn't you let me warn you? Or better yet, how did you not figure it out?" Douglas sat back in the wingback chair he always took in Colden's room.

"I knew something was off, I was just too . . . I don't know what, but I didn't want to believe what my brain was trying to tell me. Then Icelyn showed up and ran off. And I realized my mistake. You know what happened next, and now she wants out."

"Maybe you should have thought about that before making finding you a spouse a competition." Douglas rolled his eyes.

"I get that you're annoyed with me, but you don't have to be quite so obvious about it." Colden sat, sinking into his chair. He stared at the roaring fire in front of him without really seeing it.

"You made a mistake. Have you decided what you're going to do to fix it? Like maybe call off the competition."

Colden dragged his eyes away from the fire to look at his friend. "I can't do that. I made a commitment. As prince, I need to uphold it, no matter the outcome."

"Not even when it's one of the most ridiculous things you've done?"

"Not even then, because it's not all that ridiculous. I still need to know who has been making all the cocoa that makes me feel all the things. How can I marry if I don't know who that person is?" Colden ran his hands through his hair.

"Right, you don't know who this person is, but that you're willing to give up what you know is a good thing to find out. It's not a good look, Your Highness. And how do you think it made Icelyn feel? You two have just started seeing each other, and just started figuring out what it is that draws you two towards each other. And you are willing to throw it away to meet a stranger? Gods, Colden, were you trying to make Icelyn feel insignificant? Pretty sure it's going to be rough for her to forgive you."

"Oh my gods, I'm a horrible person. I didn't even think—" Colden sank down even deeper into his chair. His self-pity seemed to waft off him in waves.

"Quit feeling sorry for yourself and figure out what you can do to make it better. Remember, this is about her feelings, not yours."

The day was perfect. Icelyn closed her eyes and lifted her face towards the sky. The sun's warmth caressed her cheeks. It contrasted with the crisp, cold air and the smell of snow and pine. Her two favorite scents represented her favorite time of year. She loved how the chilly weather contrasted with the warmth of sitting fireside with a cup of hot cocoa.

"Hi, Icelyn, are you ready for the snowball battle?"

Icelyn turned to see Envi at the counter of her hot cocoa booth. Envi's black hair peeked out of her cap, a stark contrast to her pale skin and red lips. Icelyn smiled; her booth wouldn't have been as successful without the newcomer's help.

"I guess, it's most people's favorite event. I've never really understood it." Icelyn continued to mix the peanut butter chocolate mixture for her specialty hot cocoa of the day.

"I've never been: this is my first Snow Solstice Festival."

"I keep forgetting that you just moved here, I feel like I've known you forever." She poured a mug of the peanut butter hot cocoa and handed it to Envi.

"That's so nice of you, I still feel so new. But it's only been a couple of months. Plenty of time to settle in," Envi said, taking a sip of cocoa. "This might be my favorite yet. I love the contrast between the salty peanut butter and the sweetness of the chocolate, with just a hint of the bitterness dark chocolate brings with it. I don't know how you come up with these unique spins on hot cocoa."

"Not many people can pinpoint the balance of flavors I'm going for. It's nice to know someone notices. As for where I get my ideas, sometimes they just come to me, other times I go through my mother's recipe book." Icelyn took the pot from the stove and poured it into a chocolate pot. It was so much easier to serve that way. Serving from the pots always made such a mess. "She had so many amazing recipes and they all have memories attached to them. Those are actually my favorite to make and normally the most popular. I think it's because they are more than a recipe; they represent a place and time of happiness and love for me, and that goes into the making of it.

"Listen to me go on and on. You should go enter the snowball battle."

Envi looked over to the field. Icelyn followed her gaze. There were so many people bundled in their winter clothes, stretching, jumping up and down, running in place—all to get ready for the battle ahead. In front of them were piles of snowballs ready to be used in the attack. It was all a bit much for Icelyn. It was so easy for the event to go from a fun activity to something much more intense and unpleasant.

"I think I'll watch from afar this year. But you should go. I think there's someone over there who wants to talk to you." Envi nodded to the corner of the field.

Icelyn looked over and sighed. There Colden was, standing there, waiting for the event to start. She could see him scan the crowd, searching. Envi was probably right; it was more than possible he wanted to talk to her. The question was, did she want to talk to him? She hadn't forgiven him, at least not yet. But she was to the point where she was ready to listen. She scanned the crowd until her eyes found two redheads behind a large pile of snowballs. Holly saw her and waved her over.

"Are you sure you don't want to join?" Icelyn asked Envi.

"Of course, you go. I'll watch the booth while you're gone. I'm sure it will be pretty slow until after the battle."

"True." She looked over at the field with hesitation. "Are you sure you're okay staying here?"

"Yes, now go." Envi pushed her out from behind the booth and towards the prince.

"Okay, I'm going, I'm going." Icelyn laughed as she made her way through the crowd outside of the field, every one of them bundled up in warm woolen coats as the days kept getting colder as the end of the fair and Solstice grew closer.

"Over here, Icelyn," Holly called out.

Icelyn made her way over to the tower of snowballs Douglas and Holly had staked out as her sprite of a friend jumped up and down to get her attention. Icelyn waved back.

"Hi, you two, are you warmed up for the event?" Icelyn asked.

"Of course, we are, what do you think we've been doing?" Holly posed like she was going to throw a snowball.

"You do look warmed up." Icelyn's eyes darted to where the prince was standing by himself. She looked back at her friends to see Douglas watching her.

"You should go talk to him," Douglas said.

"I don't know." Icelyn hesitated.

"Trust me, go talk to him. You don't have to forgive him, but it won't hurt to listen to him."

"I guess." She turned towards the prince. Maybe she should hear him out? Her feet moved towards him, one step in front of another, moving as if she was being pulled towards him, not of her own volition.

Colden looked up at her, causing her to hesitate for a moment. He took a step forward, and she shook her head, then continued to move towards him. It was mere moments before she was standing in front of him. She tilted her head back to look up at him.

"So, I hear you want to talk. So, you should talk." Icelyn crossed her arms across her chest.

"I have so much to say."

An errant snowball came out of nowhere, smacking the prince in the face. The shocked look on his face was so comical Icelyn couldn't help but laugh. She tried to stop to say something, but the laughter continued until tears were running down her face.

"Oh, you think that's funny, do you?" He reached behind him. And came back with a giant snowball.

Her laughter stopped, and her eyes widened. He wouldn't dare. She watched as his arm drew back. His arm arched over his head, and he released the packed snow into the air, tossing it at her head. She ducked to the side before it hit her in the face. She laughed even harder. In fact, she laughed so hard she fell into the snow.

"Serves you right," Colden said, offering her an arm.

Icelyn took it, and instead of helping herself up, she pulled him down into the snow with her, laughing until she realized he was basically on top of her, his face mere inches from hers. The laughter stopped. She looked into his icy-blue eyes, then down to his lips. She licked her lower lip as the warmth of their breath mingled with the cold air.

"I want to kiss you, but only if you want me to," whispered Colden.

Did she want him to? Before the masquerade the answer would have been a definitive yes; she had looked forward to continuing what they had started in the ice maze. But now? Now she wasn't sure if he knew or cared for her at all. Was she just another woman throwing herself into his arms, and this was a convenient moment, a moment that felt like a kiss was right, needed even?

She nodded, her movements barely perceptible. Colden lowered his head slowly, giving her plenty of time to say something, anything, to stop him. She said nothing. His warm lips pressed against hers and she sighed. It felt as if she had been waiting for this moment for a lifetime. She wrapped her arms around his neck as the kiss deepened.

"Oh my gods! This can't be happening. Why does she get everything?" Stacey whined from somewhere nearby.

"I know, sister, she has a knack for ruining good things," Dru comforted, a sneer in his tone. "Maybe it's time to show her how it feels."

Icelyn broke off the kiss. "Dammit, what are they going to do to me now?" She pushed Colden off her, stood, and walked away.

"Icelyn! Wait up," Holly yelled after her.

Icelyn stopped as her friend ran up to her. Holly stopped in front of her, panting. Bending over with her hands on her knees, she held one hand up. It was dramatic enough Icelyn almost started laughing at her.

"Why . . . are . . . you . . . running . . . off?" Holly asked as she gulped down air.

"I kissed Colden in front of everyone."

"What? But that's not a bad thing. Unless you didn't want to."

"I wanted to, but I didn't want Dru and Stacey to see. And they did." Icelyn turned to Holly. "What do you think they are going to do to me now?"

"They shouldn't do anything to you. You're just living your own life. It doesn't affect them," Holly said.

"But Stacey and Dru both think they are going to capture the prince. They just see me as someone in the way, so they'll try to remove me before they accept he's not interested in either one of them," she explained.

Holly stopped. "You know they are completely disconnected from reality, right?"

"Of course, they are, but that doesn't mean they won't try to get back at me. The two of them have blamed me for everything ever since we met.

"I need to get away and think. I'm going to go for a walk. Can you make sure Envi has enough help at the cocoa booth?"

"Are you sure? I can go with you." Holly looked concerned.

Icelyn glanced towards the woods. "Yeah, I can use some alone time."

She meandered into the woods, taking in a deep breath of the crisp, cold pine scent. She watched the light filter through the trees and sparkle off the snow as she walked. It reminded her of the magical fairyland her mother would tell her stories about. Her mind wandered from the stories to her cookbook. This past week had been so much fun using recipes she hadn't used for years. She was excited to put them on her regular menu once her shop was up and running. It felt good to plan for the future. A future that may or may not include the prince.

Icelyn admitted to herself that she was falling for him. He just wasn't falling for her. She knew he liked her, but it wasn't enough for him to recognize that someone wasn't her, or to make decisions that led him to her.

"I could just enter the contest. I have a good shot at winning. My recipes have won the last few years, even if it was someone else saying the hot cocoas were theirs," Icelyn said to herself as she walked along the path.

A rustle behind her interrupted her thoughts. Before she could turn around, a hood was over her head. Everything went dark. She stopped moving. Someone threw her over their shoulder, knocking the wind out of her. She screamed, hitting whoever held her.

"Hold still. If you don't, I'm going to drop you."

"Dru?" Icelyn asked.

"Do you have her?" Stacey asked.

"No, she won't stop wiggling. I'm going to drop her," he complained.

"Let me go! Why are you doing this?" Icelyn yelled, twisting and turning, trying to escape as she did so.

"You're in our way."

Pain exploded throughout the back of her head, and the world faded away.

Chapter Twenty-Six

Colden stopped in front of Holly. "Have you seen Icelyn recently? She ran off earlier and I really was hoping to talk to her."

"She went into the forest after the twins saw you two together. She went for a walk to clear her head. I haven't seen her since," Holly answered.

"I'm going to see if I can find her. If you see her, can you let her know I want to talk?" Colden looked towards the forest. It would be dark soon. He hoped she was already back home. "Douglas, can you check to see if she's home? I'm going into the forest first."

"Of course."

Colden followed the path Holly indicated Icelyn had taken. The dark and the cold creeped in as he walked through the woods. Colden felt his pace accelerate as his earlier concern turned to something closer to a panic. He called her name as he frantically searched the different paths of the forest. Icelyn was nowhere to be found. He came across a small opening on the trail. The snow looked like there had been a scuffle where someone had been dragged off. Colden heard a rustle off of the trail.

"Who's there?" Colden asked, his head whipping back and forth as he looked all around him.

Out of the brush flew Ember. She flapped her wings and landed in front of Colden. The little dragon stomped her feet and pointed to the drag marks. Then Ember started following them. Stopping briefly, it looked like she wanted him to follow her. Colden shrugged; the dragon looked like she knew where she was going, so he followed her. The urgency he felt from Icelyn's dragon matched his own. He followed until they were outside of Mother Maude's Tea and Coffee House.

"What are we doing here, Ember?" Colden looked over at the dragon. "I don't think Icelyn would come here. I don't think she really gets along with anyone in this building. Aren't the twins continually sabotaging her?"

Ember tapped her little dragon feet in the snow and let out a puff of steam. She flew up to him and nudged him towards the door. Colden had never seen Ember act so insistent.

"Fine, I'll go in. But I really don't want to." Colden sighed. Then squared his shoulders. He raised his hand to enter the gloomy cave of a restaurant . . .

"Colden! Did you find her? She wasn't home, she wasn't anywhere I looked, and I'm really worried about her. This isn't like her at all. She left Envi in charge of the booth, promising to come back. Well, she did send me back, but then she never came back. And now it's dark." Holly's monologue stopped so she could take a deep breath.

Douglas wrapped his arm around Holly, and she burrowed into his side. Colden looked at the two of them, almost jealous of the instant connection that had formed between them. They seemed to understand each other naturally, and here he was floundering constantly. He felt like he was always messing things up.

"Why were you going in there? Icelyn would never choose to go into Mother Maude's, not after all the years of being treated the way she was. I'd give Maude a piece of my mind if Icelyn would let me." Holly glared at the door.

"Ember led me here. What do you mean by terrible treatment?" Colden asked.

Holly sighed. "That's really for Icelyn to tell you. I'm just glad she finally left the place and started her own shop. Being trapped in that dark kitchen isn't good for anyone."

"So, what's the plan?" Douglas interrupted.

"I hadn't really come up with one. I was just going to walk in and see where that led me," Colden said. Although saying it aloud had him questioning the wisdom behind it.

"I think that's a start, allow for some reconnaissance. Hopefully figure out where she is if she's in there." Douglas went into planning mode. "Do you know any secret spots or hidden rooms in the restaurant, Holly?"

Holly tapped her finger on her lower lip. "It's been years since I've been there, but I think there's a small room next to the cellar. Icelyn took me down there once. It was where she slept when her father was out of town, and Maude opened Icelyn's room up to travelers. That woman, she's the worst."

Colden couldn't believe what he was hearing. These were people respected around town. How could they treat another person so poorly? "They kept her in the cellar? Why hasn't she said anything about it? Does her father know?"

"He doesn't. She didn't want to tell him after her mother left. He tried so hard to find someone who would take care of her. She couldn't tell him that he had failed. She was also worried if she said anything, it would get worse. There were times she was locked in that small room without any interaction with others and barely any food. She never said how long they would keep her in there, but I think it was for days." Holly sniffed as her eyes filled with tears. "They almost always did that if we stayed out too late. You don't think she's there now, do you?"

"Only one way to find out." With that, Colden pushed open the door.

"Shut up, Stacey! Your constant yammering is going to wake her up. And I'd prefer she be locked away before that happens."

"There's no need to yell at me, Dru. Keep it up and you'll only have yourself to blame if she wakes up."

Icelyn's head felt as if someone had taken a cast iron pan and smashed it against her skull. The throbbing at the base of her skull made her want to go back to sleep, or faint, or do something that prevented her from feeling the pain. But that wasn't an option. Apparently, her brilliant step-siblings were kidnapping her.

Dru took a step down and his bony shoulder jabbed her hard enough to knock all the air out of her lungs. It was all she could do to stay silent as Dru continued to take steps down. She thought about fighting, but she was afraid he would drop her all the way down the stairs. Not a good feeling since her head already felt like she had been dropped down a flight of stairs. If the twins were taking her where she thought they were, it wouldn't be too hard to get out. She'd done it most of her life. It was the main reason she was staying quiet. She assumed Stacey and Dru would be less careful with securing her if they believed she had passed out. At least, that's what had happened in the past.

"How long are we going to keep her?" Stacey asked.

"Long enough to win the hot cocoa competition," Dru said. "We need to keep her away from the prince. She's woven some sort of web around the prince."

"I know." Stacey stomped her foot. "I can't believe he kissed her. Right there in the middle of the snowball battle. What does he see in her? He should be paying attention to me. And he's not." Stacey whined.

"He should be interested in one of us, at the very least." Dru grunted as he tossed Icelyn onto a pile of pillows.

The impact rattled Icelyn's teeth. Pain burst through her head. It was so sharp it felt like she could see the pain behind her eyelids. It was all she could do not to scream out from it. She couldn't believe this was all about her relationship with the prince. They were so out of touch with what was going on; they didn't even realize the prince had no interest in either one of them. She wasn't sure he was actually interested in her, but she knew he didn't enjoy being around either of them.

"Don't forget to lock the door, Stacey. We need to keep her here until after the competition. We can't win if she enters," Dru said.

"Why do you always assume I'm going to forget and mess things up? I'm so sick of you telling me what to do and second-guessing me. I'm the one who cut all the dragon's leashes so the captain of the guard couldn't blame us for Ember's disappearance. Stealing the dress worked out. And Prince Colden enjoyed spending time with me until he realized I wasn't her. I was making real progress," Stacey rattled on.

Of course, it was her, Icelyn thought as she listened to the twins' fight.

"And whose idea was it to steal the dress? Mine. You wouldn't have been with him all night if it wasn't for me. And I got stuck on the sidelines while you got to have all the fun."

Icelyn heard the door close. She waited to hear if Stacey remembered to lock the door. There was no click of a lock or a deadbolt turning. Nothing. Icelyn sighed, thankful Stacey always forgot to do things. She waited until the voices of Dru and Stacey disappeared before she moved at all. Removing the hood, she got up off the ground and looked around her. Like she thought, she was in her old room. She couldn't count the number of times she had snuck out of here. It was just a matter of waiting long enough for Dru and Stacey to get bored keeping watch. If it was just Stacey, she would only have to wait about an hour or two. Dru was always a bit more tenacious. She brushed off her skirt and sat down on the pillows. It was time to wait out Dru.

She woke up with a start. Her head hurt slightly less than before, but it was still an instant reminder of why she was down in the cellar. Her ridiculous step-siblings, that's why. She listened to see if she could hear anything happening on the stairs or above. Everything sounded calm. She slowly opened the door, peering outside. No one was there. A sigh of relief escaped before she made her way upstairs.

The door at the top of the stairs burst open. Her heart dropped into her stomach and her palms started to sweat. Why would Dru and Stacey be coming back now? She must have been down there for hours. Icelyn pressed herself up against the wall as if that would make anyone coming down the stairs not see her standing there. She was literally right in front of them.

"Icelyn, you're safe," Colden said.

"Colden . . . What are you doing here?" She stepped away from the wall. Two more people came through the door. "And Holly, Douglas? Why?"

"I'm—We're here to rescue you." Colden looked around sheepishly.

Chapter Twenty-Seven

Icelyn walked out of the cave-like restaurant she had spent her childhood in with Colden by her side and her friends behind her. It felt good to have their support. This was the first time she had walked out of the building and not felt alone. Yes, Holly had always been there for her, but she snuck out to see Holly, knowing Maude would catch her and punish her at least half the time. This time she was walking out with her friends, and she wasn't going to be punished for it. At least, not the ways she was punished before.

"Do you know why they took you?" Colden asked as they walked to her cottage.

"The same reason they blamed me for the snow falling from the tree and cut the dragon's leashes."

In her peripheral, Icelyn saw Colden glance over his shoulder and nod at Douglas as if telling him to take note as he said to her, "And that is . . ."

Icelyn looked over at the prince. "Um . . . Well . . ." She hesitated. "That is, they think I'm getting in the way of you choosing them . . . one of them."

His head snapped towards her. "Choose one of them? I would never choose one of them."

"I know that, but that's not something you would ever convince them of." Icelyn rolled her eyes.

Colden just stared for a moment. "Why would they even think they had a chance? I haven't spoken to them the entire event."

"Other than at the masquerade, when you spent the evening with Stacey?" Her feet moved faster, as if she was trying to escape the memory of the other night.

The prince sped up to keep up with her. "I'm sorry. I assumed it was you. Why would anyone else have the dress I gave you? It's not an excuse. Things felt off, but I thought it was all in my head."

"I get it, whatever. It's done and over." She crossed her arms, withdrawing into herself.

"But you don't. I wanted to spend the evening with you. Not anyone else. Instead, I was with a poor substitution, and I hurt you because I was—" He paused. "I don't even know how to put it into words—unwilling to see what was in front of me."

"I told you it's fine." If they kept talking, she was going to cry. She didn't feel like crying right now. It was too cold. And her day had been trying enough so far. "I just want to go home and sleep."

Colden stopped her. "I have a better idea. Come with me."

"I'm tired. I don't want any more adventure today."

"This will be worth it. Trust me." Colden waved Douglas over. "Just wait here for a moment, please." He pleaded before leaving her standing alone while he talked with his guard.

Icelyn sighed. It was hard for her to say no to someone who wanted to cheer her up. Even if it meant he wasn't really listening to her. The men stopped whispering and Douglas took off, leaving Holly in the street.

"What are you up to?" she asked as Colden sauntered towards her. There was a newfound confidence in his step. *Whatever he's planning must be good, at least in his mind,* she thought.

He took her hand. Warmth radiated through his gloves and hers as he held on to her. "It's a surprise. I know you're going to love it. If you'll give me a chance after the other night."

She should say no: her day hadn't been easy, she was tired, and she still had to prep for tomorrow. Instead, her head nodded up and down. He pulled her towards him, wrapping his arms around her as their bodies touched from chest to knees. He picked her up and spun her around before taking her hand once again and dashing through the village towards something. At least she hoped it was something.

He stopped in front of a stunning black-and-silver carriage with dappled grey horses already harnessed in. "Your carriage, milady." He bowed with a grand swoosh of his arm.

Icelyn climbed the steps into the open-air carriage, taking the fur blankets and tucking them around her as soon as she sat. Colden slid into the seat next to her, his side pressed to hers. His warmth made it seem much warmer than it actually was. He looked towards her before picking up the reins.

It soon was clear they were headed to the palace, but there was no indication of why. Instead of worrying about what was going on, she snuggled into the blankets and Colden's side, enjoying the moment for what it was. A moment where she didn't have to be in control, she could watch the trees go by and enjoy the moon and the stars above, without having to worry. The rocking of the carriage and the lack of concern for almost anything had her drifting off to sleep before long.

"Wake up, Icelyn," Colden whispered, kissing her on her forehead.

She stretched groggily. "Where are we?"

"The palace. Come on, I can't wait for you to see." Colden grabbed her hand and started to run. They turned the corner into the ice arena where the masquerade was held.

It somehow looked like the other night, and nothing like the other night. Candles glowed around the outskirts of the ice. In the corner, there was a roaring fire in the oversized fireplace with fur boots lined up in front of it. In front of that was a table set for two. On the dais stood a female singer decked out in a green wool, the warmth of the candles bringing out the deeper red color in her auburn hair. Next to her was Douglas on the lute. Behind them was the rest of the band.

"Let's put on some skates," Colden said.

"You don't have to do this," Icelyn said. Nothing would make the sting of the other night disappear except the fading away of time.

"This isn't about whether or not I have to do something. This is about doing what I want, not what is needed," Colden whispered into her ear. "Come, let's put on some skates."

She followed Colden to the oversized fireplace. There, he indicated with a nod that she should sit. She watched as he raced off to get skates, his smile so big she felt her lips start to turn up in a smile, like his enjoyment of the moment was contagious. It wasn't long before he came back with two pairs of skates. He knelt down in front of her and picked up her right foot, carefully removing her winter boot. His hand lightly caressed her leg as he did so, causing her skin to tingle under his warm touch. All she could do was watch as he took great care putting the skate on her foot and tying it so it was neither too loose nor too tight. He repeated the process with her left foot, making her feel all warm and fuzzy. She watched as he quickly put on his skates and stood, holding his hands out towards her. Without any hesitation, she took them, and they made their way to the ice together.

Icelyn stepped on the ice and glided to a stop in front of the prince. It had been a while since she'd skated: starting the café had consumed all of her time. Being on the ice reminded her of her favorite times with her family, and later, when she snuck out to see Holly. She felt her smile grow as the memories washed over her. Before Colden could do anything other than admire her smile, she pushed off and made her way over the ice, twirling and cutting back and forth, her feet moving in familiar patterns. When she was in front of the prince again, she stopped, spraying him with ice.

"This is what the other night was supposed to be like. You and me, and your happiness wafting off you in waves." He looked over at the dais and nodded. Douglas started to play, and before long, the singer's voice penetrated the air as she sang a Snow Solstice carol.

"But the other day, we wouldn't have been alone," Icelyn said.

Colden's arm slipped around her waist until they stood side by side. He bent over and whispered, "It would have felt like we were alone. No one else would have mattered. As we twirled around the ice, they would have disappeared until it felt like only the two of us were left."

She shivered as his breath caressed her ear, or maybe it was because of the intimacy of his words. She could feel what he was talking about. The crowd becoming unimportant. Each of them only focusing on the other. It was enough to make her heart go pitter-patter. She didn't know how long they glided across the ice, but they stopped eventually, and Colden escorted her to the solitary table. One of the wait staff from the other night served fried pastry sticks with sipping cocoa.

"How . . . ?" she started to ask.

"The sous chef was so impressed with what was made the other night she committed it to memory. I asked her to recreate it."

"But I . . ."

"Shhhh, just try it," Colden interrupted, holding out a bite for her to take.

Unable, or maybe just unwilling to refuse, she took a bite. She closed her eyes, letting just the scent, the feel, and the flavor of the dessert envelop her senses. It was good. The dough was both crispy on the outside and custard-like in the center. The chocolate mint sipping cocoa was rich and bright. It was quite good, almost as good as hers. Impressive, considering the sous chef had only seen it made the one time. She was very talented.

"Let's get these skates off." Colden pulled her chair out and escorted her closer to the fire. He once again knelt before her, undoing her skates, and slipping her feet into the fur-lined boots that had been warmed by the fire.

She waited while he took off his skates. Douglas and the band had disappeared at some point in the evening. It was just her and the prince. All the feelings she had been trying not to feel for the prince came crashing in on her in waves. It was true; she was falling in love with him, and tonight had just made it worse.

She watched as he stood up and offered his hand to help her up. Taking it, she pulled herself up until they were chest to chest. His eyebrow raised as her arms encircled his neck. She stood on her tiptoes and pressed her lips to his. For a brief moment, she felt his muscles tense, then his arms wrapped around her waist and lifted her up. The kiss she initiated deepened and went on until she couldn't breathe.

He set her down and took a small step back. "I want to . . .," Colden started, but trailed off.

"Yes." Icelyn barely recognized her own voice.

"Are you sure?" He held her shoulders as he stared into her eyes.

She nodded her head and took his head in her hands and kissed him again. This time softer, sweeter. She dropped back down to her flat feet. "Well, are we . . ."

That's all it took for the prince to grab her hand and dash off to his room, stopping anytime the mood to kiss struck.

Chapter Twenty-Eight

Light hit her face, waking Icelyn. She stretched before opening her eyes, not ready to start the day yet. *Wait, why was there light?* Her eyes popped open as she sat straight up. She was in the prince's room, wrapped in a luxurious fur blanket, sitting on the softest bed she had ever slept in. But none of that mattered: she was late. She had nothing prepped for today, no pastries made, not even a specialty hot cocoa picked out for the day. The prince rolled over and snuggled into her side, tempting her to continue to lie in bed next to him. Instead, she jumped out of bed, taking one of the many blankets with her. Where were all her clothes? She wrapped the blanket around her, covering herself as she frantically looked around the room. There they were strewn across the floor. It took mere moments for her to shimmy into her pink wool dress.

She looked over at the bed to see Colden's blue eyes watching her. She tucked her hair behind her ears and looked away. His attention—anyone's attention—was not something she was used to and it was embarrassing for her.

"Come back, Icelyn." Colden reached out towards her.

She continued to get dressed, adding one layer after another because she knew outside was going to be frigid. "I can't. I should already be working. Normally my booth would be open already, and I don't even have anything made for today. I have to go."

"But staying would be so much more fun. Are you sure you can't stay?"

"I'm positive. I have to get to work. Now." She could feel panic starting to work its way into her brain, setting off her fight-or-flight instincts. Flight was winning at the moment.

Colden stood and walked over to her. He took her into his arms. "It's going to be fine. I'll call a carriage for you." He lifted her chin and kissed her.

She stepped out of his embrace. "Thank you, I really appreciate it."

"I can come with you," he offered.

"It's okay; I'm sure you have princely things to take care of. I just need to get back. I'll see you tomorrow." She stood on her tiptoes and kissed his cheek before leaving his room.

Icelyn made her way through the castle, attempting to be as quiet as she possibly could. It wasn't until she was down the stairs and out the front door that she let out her breath. The clip-clop of the horse's hooves let her know the carriage was close. As soon as it pulled in front of her, she climbed in and bundled herself up in the provided blankets. The sway of the carriage calmed her nerves, and before she knew it, she was in front of her café.

She jumped down from the carriage and waved goodbye to the driver as he drove away. It was nice to be back in her world instead of the magical world of the palace. Holly stood across the street watching Ember and some other pet dragons play at the park.

"Oh Holly, you're such a darling friend. Thank you so much for taking care of Ember last night." Icelyn hugged her friend.

Holly stepped back. "It's about time you got home. I've been waiting all night to hear about what happened. How could you leave me wondering for so long?"

Icelyn spun, then laughed at herself for her exuberant behavior. "It was the perfect evening. He took me ice skating and had the kitchen make the dessert I made the night before. It was so cozy with the fire roaring and . . . well . . . just magical."

"Sounds like things have progressed past the helping-each-other stage and into something real," Holly said.

"I hope so. I know it's silly, but I'm going to enter the contest. He still doesn't know it was me that made the sipping chocolate the other night. I'm sure to win, and it will be such a surprise."

"Or you could just tell him, and this whole contest could be forgotten and put into the past." Holly waved Ember over so they could head to the café.

"What's the fun in that?" Icelyn danced across the street; nothing could bring her down today. At least that's what she thought—

—until she saw the café's front door cracked open about an inch. The door should have been closed and locked. Holly took Ember home from the hot cocoa booth yesterday, and she was the one who locked the door. Not that there was much to protect, just the cashbox and her mother's recipes. As soon as the thought entered her head, she knew . . . Dru and Stacey had struck again.

She yanked the door open and stepped inside. Things looked . . . normal. Still in disarray from the last incident, but her ingredients were all in place. All her mugs looked to be in one piece. She shook her head. There was no way the door was open and nothing had happened in here. She crept towards the checkout area, where she kept the cash box and recipes. Sure enough, the bejeweled box her mother had left her was gone. Even worse, all her recipes, all her mother's recipes, everything she used to make her hot cocoa . . . gone. She sank to the floor and cried.

The jangle of the doorbell halted her tears for a minute. Glancing towards the door, she saw the vague outline of a redheaded mountain man entering her shop. She wiped away the tears that obscured her vision so she could confirm it was only Douglas before she went back to her sulking.

"What happened now?" Douglas asked.

Icelyn tried to tell him what happened, but just trying to say the words out loud caused her to sob. Her words were unintelligible.

"Icelyn, sweetie. You have to calm down so you can tell us what happened."

Holly plopped down next to her. She felt Holly's arm wrap around her shoulder. Instead of calming down, she cried more into her friend's shoulder, unable to be anything but a blubbering mess. At some point, she calmed down. At least enough to tell Douglas what happened. As soon as she finished talking, waves of loss and sadness wafted over her again. The box itself was a gift from her mother as was the recipe book. Those were the only two things she owned to remember her mother by, and now they were both gone. She should never have kept them together.

Douglas crouched down next to her and Holly. "Can I please go have a word with the twins now?" he asked, desperate to put a stop to this.

"Why bother? They aren't going to be happy until I leave this place." How they treated her had always walked the line of decency, crossing over here and there, but this was beyond anything they had ever done before.

" 'Why bother?' Did you really just ask that, Icelyn?" Douglas threw up his hands. "You can't let them get away with this. The more they get away with, the more crap like this they are going to pull. They sabotaged the dragon race. They kidnapped you. For the love of the gods, they need to be stopped!"

"But how are you going to stop them? Throw them in the dungeon? I don't want anything like that. I just want to be able to live out my life without them interfering."

"They couldn't interfere if they were in the dungeon," Holly muttered.

"It doesn't matter where they are now. I can't make any of the different cocoas for the shop because I don't have the list of ingredients. Or what makes it magical." Icelyn sighed as a single tear fell from her eyes.

"You know it's not your mom's recipes that make your hot cocoa magical. It's you, and it's always been you. You're so happy making it and everyone that takes a sip can feel it. You don't need a recipe book for that, because it's all you." Holly disentangled herself from the comforting hug to look her straight in the eye. When Icelyn looked away, Holly took her by the chin, insisting on eye contact. "Do you understand me?"

Icelyn heard what her friend was saying. She just didn't have it in her to believe any of it. This past week had done her in. There were too many highs, followed by too many lows. She was done, ready to pack it all up and throw in the towel. Dru and Stacey won. They could own the only café in Wynterfell; they could have the prince . . . The prince, that's what started this entire thing. Nothing truly destructive had happened to her prior to her coming back to the café wearing the prince's cloak. She shook her head and wiped the tears from her eyes. If she wanted to keep her business, she knew what she had to do.

"It's because of my relationship with the prince. That's why they are doing this to me," she muttered.

"Even more reason to let me do something about it. Colden would order me to if he knew those two were torturing you because he showed interest. In fact, I am going to do something. This is royal business now." Douglas turned to leave, but Icelyn stopped him before he could take a step.

"No, I can make it all go away. It's not like our relationship was real, anyway." She sniffed, ignoring the intruding thoughts of their magical night and morning.

Chapter Twenty-Nine

"Don't do it, Icelyn." Holly glared at her. "Don't give up your relationship with the prince because of your step-siblings. You've already dealt with enough of their crap. Now it's time for you to take what you want."

"If only it was that easy. It seems like I don't get to have it all. I can have a quiet life and run my café, or I can have the prince. I'm sure I would have to give up the café if I married him, anyway. No one wants a queen that's in trade." Icelyn looked around until she found her stack of paper and quill pen.

Douglas snatched the pen out of her hand. "You don't know that. I'm sure Colden would never ask you to give up something you love so much. And I can stop the twins. You just need to let them get what's coming to them. They've committed crimes. Multiple. I'm more than happy to throw them in prison and toss the key."

"You can't do that." Icelyn tried to take her pen back, but he just stood there, dangling it over her head, out of reach. "Give me my pen back."

She jumped up trying to grab the pen out of Douglas's hand. He just moved it farther out of reach. This continued until she was out of breath. Douglas was doing his best not to laugh. It was almost working. Icelyn stopped, hands on her knees, panting.

"Can you please explain to me why I can't put a couple of criminals in jail? At least for the night. It would be so satisfying to scare them." Douglas lowered the pen as he talked.

She snatched it out of his hand. "I can't do it. They may be a terrible family, but they are my family. I can't be the one responsible for their demise."

Douglas looked at her, then his empty hand, and back at her. Holly patted his shoulder to comfort him.

"She's always been a wily one, Douglas," Holly said.

"That's not it . . . I mean it is . . . She snatched that pen when the moment arrived. But really, I'm more disturbed by her insistence on protecting two people who would probably run her over with a carriage if given the opportunity." He threw up his hands and walked to the front door. "The prince has never been happier than he is now. Something changed in him when he met you. He smiles more. This thing between the two of you, it's not fake. I don't think it ever really was. He would do anything for you. Don't throw it away to save two people who would rather lock you in a cellar than see you happy." With that final word, he turned and left.

"He's not wrong, you know," Holly said.

Icelyn stared at the paper in front of her, unable to look at her friend, the only person who knew what she had gone through with Maude and the twins. "I know he's not wrong. But is he right? Is it that black and white, or are there shades of grey? I just know that I can't be the reason those two get their comeuppance. I can't do that to my father. He tried to do the right thing. If he knew how bad it was for me it would kill him, and the guilt would overwhelm me."

"You have nothing to feel guilty about. You are not in control of their actions. Only they are, and those two are awful. They always have been." Holly gave her a quick hug. "Before you go and throw away your happiness, you need to ask yourself if they're worth it. Think about what your father would want for you. I'm sure he would rather you be happy than never find out about his second family. You might also want to think about whether or not this will actually make them stop. You seem to forget all the stuff they did before you met the prince."

Icelyn watched her friend walk out of the café, Holly's words echoing in her head, making her question whether or not she should write to the prince. Was she giving up her happiness for Dru and Stacey? Would the twins leave her alone if she wasn't spending time with the prince? Or was she protecting herself and everything she had worked so hard to create? Did she really think the twins would stop bothering her if she only had her café? She didn't have the answers to any of those questions, but she did know she felt a deep need to be in control. So, she did the one thing she could do. She sat down and started to write.

Dear Prince Colden,

Honestly, I don't know how to start this letter; especially after last night. Last night was absolutely magical. Which is why it pains me to write this.

She tapped the quill on her teeth. Was that the right way to start this? She didn't know. Maybe she shouldn't be writing it at all.

When I got back to my place today, it had been burglarized yet again. This time, what was stolen is irreplaceable. As I was sitting there, crying over my loss, I once again realized none of this was happening before I began to spend time with you. In fact, every time I've been seen with you, something bad has happened to me, or my shop, or Ember. I'm sorry, but I can't handle it anymore. The twins win, at least this very small battle. I can't be with you. I hope you find someone else that makes you happy.

Yours, Icelyn

She folded up the letter, put it in an envelope, and carefully wrote his name on it. Looking at the finished letter in her hand, she questioned whether or not she should send it again.

"What do you think, Ember? Will our lives be better or worse if I send this letter breaking it off with the prince?"

Ember's head rose from her bed in front of the fire. She blinked twice, stood, circled around in her bed three times, and lay back down in a tiny bun-like shape, her little nose tucked under her wing.

"I'm not really sure how to take that. Is one blink for yes and two for no? Or is it the other way around?" She sighed. "Absolutely no help at all."

The bell above her door rang.

"Holly, I'm not in the mood to talk anymore," Icelyn said as she laid her head down on the counter.

"Sorry to disappoint, but I'm not Holly."

Icelyn popped up from her seat. "I'm so sorry. How can I help you, Tasha?"

"Looks like you're the one that needs help today. I saw the closed sign at the booth and wanted to make sure you were okay. Clearly, you're not. What's going on?" Tasha pulled a chair over to the counter to sit with her.

"Life decision time."

"It doesn't look like you're very happy to make this decision. And from everything Envi has told me, things have been busy at the festival booth. Lines all day long. She may have even mentioned a romantic interlude and the snowball fight with the prince. From what she's said, your relationship with the prince isn't so fake anymore." Tasha rattled on about all the things Icelyn should be focused on.

"My café was broken into again. This time they took things I can't replace. I think I know how to stop the culprits; but I don't really know if it will. And it means giving up on something that could be really special."

"I'm sorry." Tasha took Icelyn's hands in hers. "Is there anything I can do to help?"

"Not really. What would you do if you realized you couldn't have it all? That you had to choose between doing something you love and being with someone you love?"

"I wouldn't choose. If you want to have it all, you have to work to get it all. And make the choices that will get you there. If you're compromising, then you aren't working hard enough for what you want."

Icelyn sighed. Tasha was right, but it wasn't the answer she wanted to hear. Tasha's answer meant she was going to have to do something about Dru and Stacey. And she was going to have to talk to Colden about her café and how important it was to her. Fighting for what she wanted meant a lot of potential conflict, and she preferred to avoid conflict.

"Now, that's handled, even if you didn't like my answer. Do you have any baked goods available? I need to go to the castle, and I don't want to go empty-handed."

"I can make some cookies. I just need half an hour." Icelyn started gathering ingredients for her caramel apple cookies—one of her recipes, not her mother's.

"I can wait: when else will I have the chance to see you work?" Tasha sat and watched her work in the kitchen.

Icelyn felt all the sadness and loss wash away as she mixed the dry and wet ingredients together, careful to dry the diced apples as much as possible before coating them in flour and cinnamon, then adding them to the mix. It felt like mere moments before a batch of cookies were in the oven and she was working on the caramel topping.

"I've never seen anyone less stressed in the kitchen than you. It's like a new person took over your body, leaving behind the sad shell you were when I walked in." Tasha pushed her curls out of her face.

"I love baking. It has always made me happy. I know these cookies will make someone smile, which makes me smile. And a little smile can change the entire day. So, in a sense, these cookies might change someone's day." Icelyn boxed up the finished cookies and put them on the counter. "Here you go, cookies for the castle."

"Thank you so much. I'm sure Colden will love these." The bell jangled above the door as Tasha left.

Icelyn wiped down the kitchen, cleaning up the mess she had made. She then went back to the counter where she had written the letter. The letter . . . where was it? She frantically started to pick up everything on the counter. How could it have walked out of here on its own? She thought about setting the cookies down, Tasha picking them up, and realized the letter was on its way to the castle. Little did she know that her baking was going to change someone's day . . . just not for the better.

Chapter Thirty

"Oh my gods! Did you taste these cookies?" Douglas said, sending cookie crumbs across the room.

"How can you eat at a time like this?" Colden asked, shaking a piece of paper in Douglas's face.

"What do you mean, 'a time like this?'" Douglas chewed slower.

Colden felt his friend focus on him, finally sensing his distress. He held out the letter once again. Douglas snatched it from his hand. He watched as his head guard read the letter.

"She didn't." Douglas stroked his beard.

Colden swiped his hand through his hair. "She did." He plopped down in his chair. "What happened? She didn't hint at wanting to break it off this morning. Nothing."

He actually was thinking about canceling the hot cocoa competition after this morning. Icelyn was more important to him than some random person he had never met. But then he received this letter, telling him it was over.

"Her café was broken into again. This time, they stole the recipe book her mother had given her," Douglas explained as he sat in the chair across from Colden.

"Someone broke in again? And this time they took something from her that's irreplaceable and sentimental. I'm sure she's devastated. Maybe I should go to her, see if I can help." Colden stood, then sat back down. "She doesn't want my help. Instead, she wrote this letter." He shook the papers once more. "She just kicked me to the cobblestones."

He stared into the fire, wondering why being burglarized would make her split up with him. Was she somehow blaming him for what happened to her? He stopped and thought back to his time with Icelyn. Douglas told him about the destruction of her kitchen right after he had lent her his cloak. Then the café was torn apart and she had to shut down, after they walked through town. Ember went missing when they were on a sleigh ride, and now this, after he kissed her in the snowball battlefield. Not to mention the kidnapping.

Maybe this was all his fault. He sighed.

"I've caused her more problems than I'm worth. Ever since we met, she's been targeted," Colden said.

Douglas looked over, surprised. "That's very noble of you to take the blame. But you aren't out there stealing her things, cutting leashes, and kidnapping her, are you? I believe the person to blame is the one committing those awful acts."

"But she wouldn't have been a target if it wasn't for me. Sometimes I wish I wasn't a prince; that I wasn't born to be king. No one would care if I was a carpenter trying to win her heart. They would all us leave well enough alone. But as a prince, everyone cares." He slid down in his chair, arms crossed.

"Pouting is not a good look on you, Your Highness," Douglas said.

"What do you want me to do? I could sulk, is that any better than pouting? Is it more princely?" Colden tossed the words dripping with sarcasm across the room.

"I always thought of you as more of a man of action; pouting and sulking seems a bit pedestrian if you ask me."

"What am I supposed to do? She wrote a letter calling it quits. I have to respect it. It's not like I'm going to go bang on her door and force her to talk to me."

"Are you sure this is from her? It could be the twins. They are out to destroy her in any way possible," Douglas said.

"It came with baked goods that tasted good. There's no way it came from the twins. These cookies would have been terrible if they had come from them." He sighed.

Douglas laughed.

Colden glared at him. "This is no laughing matter."

"I don't know, your distaste for the twin's baking is pretty funny. Especially since they are so sure they have a chance with you."

Colden sat forward in his chair. "Do you think everything that's happened to Icelyn is coming from their belief that I would marry one of them if she wasn't around?"

"I do. But they are her step-siblings. She thinks of them as family and won't let me bring them in," Douglas said, his annoyance clear in his tone.

"I don't get it. Why would she protect them at all? Holly said they used to keep her in a locked room in the cellar. That's not a family anyone wants to be a part of or should want to be a part of." He was baffled by the information Douglas had just given him. Why would she protect people that treated her so poorly?

"You know, we could always try to catch them in the act." Douglas rubbed his hands together.

"Are you plotting? Is that a good plot I'm sensing?" He smiled at his friend's villain-like antics.

"We need to catch them in the act. I'm thinking we do it at the hot cocoa competition tomorrow."

Colden could see his friend's mind at work, coming up with some intricate plan to capture the twins. "Why the hot cocoa competition?"

Douglas looked at him as if he had taken leave of his senses. "These two want to become part of your family. They will do whatever it takes to win tomorrow. Which I'm sure means cheating."

"I would rather cancel the competition. I don't know what I was thinking when I made that announcement."

"You weren't thinking, but at least we can now use it to our advantage," Douglas said.

"But I'm not ready to marry anyone. I can see committing myself to Icelyn, but no one else, not even my fantasy cocoa maker. I can't hold a competition if I can't go through with my end of it."

Douglas laughed. "And just yesterday you were telling me you couldn't even think of canceling it because 'once royalty proclaims something, they have to follow through.' "

"I was being an ass. I'm royalty. I can do what I want." Colden crossed his arms.

"Now you're being an ass. If I promise you won't end up engaged—unless you want to—will you follow through on the competition?" Douglas pleaded.

"Fine, but it's going to be a waste."

"Okay, Pouty McPouterson, you just leave it to me; it will not be a waste. Especially if the twins get what they deserve. That, in and of itself, makes the competition worth having." Douglas grabbed his cloak.

"Is it really enough? It still leaves me marrying someone I don't want to marry."

"Just ask your father to do something, like announce whoever wins has to prove themselves before the wedding. Or maybe, trust me and see what happens." Douglas opened the door. "Oh, and if I ask you to do something tomorrow, I'm going to need you to listen and do it."

Trust his captain of the guard and best friend? Was that something he should do? Colden stared into the fire, contemplating the end of his life as he knew it.

Chapter Thirty-One

Icelyn had been sitting in her kitchen for hours, just staring at the ingredients in front of her. She didn't know what to do. Tomorrow was the last day of the festival. She needed to have a hot cocoa to serve, and it needed to be special. But how was she going to make it special without her mother's recipes? She had been using them as a basis for all her ideas her entire career.

She rolled up her sleeves so she could get to work. Instead of focusing on hot cocoa, she needed to get into the zone, and that required something a little less fancy, but something she could serve in her café. She tapped her fingers on her lips, deep in thought.

Ember dropped a bag of chocolate chips on the counter in front of her, causing her to jump at least six feet out of her chair.

"Oh, Ember," she said with a laugh. "You scared me half-to-death. I take you want me to make something with chocolate chips?"

Ember tapped her toes and flapped her wings in affirmation.

"Okay, how about puff pastry with chocolate rolled in?" She looked at Ember with a raised eyebrow.

Ember stood on the counter and blew out a puff of steam.

"I take it you're not in the mood for flaky, buttery goodness. Okay, then." She looked around and an idea hit her. A cinnamon roll, but instead of a buttery cinnamon and sugar filling, she could do a chocolate chip and peanut butter one. She was certain it would be delicious. Kinda like the hot cocoa she had last made in flavor profile, but with soft yeasted bread to add to it. She could even top it off with a banana glaze.

Ember followed her around as she gathered all the ingredients; every now and then she would flap her wings or blow out a puff of steam, depending on whether or not she approved or disapproved. But at this point, Icelyn had made up her mind. She was going to make these rolls, and they were going to be delicious.

She put all of her dry ingredients into a bowl, careful to put the yeast on the opposite side of the bowl from the salt. Mixing those two too soon would kill the yeast, and she would never get the fluffy rolls she wanted. She slowly mixed warm buttermilk into the dry mix, getting her hands dirty in the process. After the buttermilk, she added the eggs, one at a time. The dough was a little sticky once everything was incorporated, so she added a bit more flour and kneaded it all together until she could see the gluten forming. She dropped the ball of dough into an oiled bowl and covered it. The dough needed a few hours to rise before she could roll it out, add her peanut butter chocolate mixture, and make the rolls.

Icelyn sat on one of the pillows next to the fire. Ember curled up next to her, resting her cute little head in her lap. Absentmindedly, Icelyn petted the dragon until they both started to drift off to sleep. She shook her head and jumped up.

"Now is not the time to nap. I have baking to do. Ember, could you light the stove so I can start melting the peanut butter chocolate mixture for the rolls?" She washed her hands as Ember hopped over to the stove and blew enough fire to light the stove. Ember hopped back over to her, stopping when she was close enough to nuzzle her leg. She patted the dragon on the head.

"You are always the best girl, aren't you? I don't know what I would do without you. Now I need to make the filling while the dough rises so it can cool before it needs to be spread."

Icelyn grabbed butter, chocolate chips, and peanut butter and took them over to the stove. She filled a pot with water, put it on the burner, and grabbed a bowl to put over the top of it so she could melt all the ingredients together. Her feet stepped to the beat in her head, dancing as she waited for the water to boil. She sang as she mixed the three ingredients together until they were smooth. Removing the bowl, she twirled as she put it on the countertop and finished her song with a flourish. No longer singing, she could hear Ember whining. Glancing over at the dragon, she saw her hiding in a corner with her ears covered. Icelyn burst into laughter. She was a great baker, but apparently her singing left something to be desired.

"Get over here, Ember. I've stopped singing."

Ember peeked out of the corner and slowly let her arms fall to her side. She crept across the room, blew her steam puff of dissatisfaction, and curled up in her bed.

"Okay, no more singing, I get it." Icelyn grabbed the dough that had risen to twice its size, so it was time to finish her peanut butter chocolate buns. Which was exactly what she did.

She was happy as she rolled out the dough, coating the inside with filling, rolling them back up, slicing the dough into rolls, and letting them rise to get ready for the final bake. As the rolls grew in size, she mixed together a banana frosting. Just the thing to perfect the rolls. She was drooling just thinking about the mix of flavors, so it was a good thing they were ready to go into the oven. Twenty minutes later, she was pulling them out of the oven and frosting them, allowing the banana frosting to add to the delicious ooey-gooeyness in front of her.

She plated one roll while it was still warm. It smelled divine. She took a bite and her eyes fluttered shut as each of the flavors caressed her tongue and melded in her mouth. This was perfection, and she didn't have a recipe for it. Maybe she had overreacted earlier. It was still devastating that she had lost something so sentimental to her, but it didn't mean she was lost in the kitchen. She knew what she was doing, even without the recipe book sitting in the drawer next to her.

Forget the letter she wrote that accidentally made its way to the castle, forget the twins and everything they had done to her—she was going to enter the contest tomorrow, and she was going to win. She packed up three boxes of rolls and dashed off three notes. Each one with the same message: to meet at the café tomorrow morning as early as they possibly could. She had a hot cocoa contest to win, and she needed their help to make it happen.

She leaned on the counter, tapping her fingers to her lips. Should she send some to Colden as well?

"What do you think, Ember? Should I send Colden some of these rolls, or just surprise him tomorrow?" She looked over as her dragon slept by the fireplace and didn't stir one bit. She laughed; guess she was going to have to figure out what to do on her own.

She looked over at the rolls and grabbed another one while she thought about what to do. When she finished, she put them away and cleaned her kitchen.

She did not send anything up to the castle for Colden.

Chapter Thirty-Two

"Why do you have to do everything so early in the morning?" Holly complained as she stumbled through the café door. Douglas followed behind her, but where Holly looked like death walking, he looked chipper and ready to start the day.

"It's not that early, Holly," Douglas said.

"Don't." Holly held up her hand. "The sun's not out yet, and I've spent the last week waking up at this gods' awful hour so Icelyn would be a success." Holly crossed her arms. "You don't even sulk right. Shouldn't you be in bed under the covers wallowing?" She stared at Icelyn with something akin to hate in her eyes.

Icelyn laughed off her friend's grumpy mood and handed her a hot coffee beverage filled with chocolate and a touch of cayenne pepper. "Here, this will wake you up. And shut you up. That way, I can explain what's happening."

The bell above the door jangled as the last of her friends arrived. Tasha didn't look much better than Holly, with her curls piled atop her head, some sticking out in very awkward angles.

"Someone better start explaining what's going on. While I appreciate the treats, I'm not sure I like the intrigue . . . Who am I to lie? I love the intrigue; I just don't love being up this early."

"Hear, hear, soul sister." Holly raised her mug in the air.

Icelyn shoved a warm coffee into Tasha's hands. When she took a sip, a satisfied smile replaced the early morning glare.

"Yesterday, as you all know, I was devastated by the theft of my mother's recipe book. But Holly's voice was in my head, telling me over and over again that I didn't need the book, that it was all inside me. After Tasha stopped by and asked for some baked goods, I actually listened to her voice." Icelyn took a breath. "Did Colden get the letter?" she asked Douglas.

"He did. Were you planning on breaking him? Because yesterday he was pretty broken."

"I didn't mean for him to even see the letter. It accidentally ended up with the caramel apple cookies. I almost sent him another letter, but I figured I could fix everything if I just win the contest today. My recipes have won the last five years, so there's no reason I won't win today."

Holly jumped up and down as Icelyn finished her speech. "Finally, some gumption. I'm so sick of those fools walking all over you. Let's do this. What exactly are we doing?"

"We're helping her win the competition, that's what we're doing," Tasha said.

"And you get an inside look for the *Tattler* if you want it," Icelyn said.

Tasha blushed. "That's really nice of you, but honestly, I would rather just see you win. Just keep me on as the royal reporter once you're queen."

Icelyn laughed. "Is that even a thing? Anyway, we need to get to work if I'm going to make this happen. Douglas, what's Colden's favorite hot cocoa?"

"Hmmm, I think it's anything you do with peppermint. That's when he makes his worst decisions because he feels like he's in love with the person who made it. Which he is, but he doesn't know that yet. It's funny to watch him act all lovesick—until he makes a proclamation that could ruin his life."

"I don't really understand how he hasn't figured out that it's me. Anyway, that's my favorite as well, so I think that's the perfect one to make." Icelyn paced. "I need ingredients, specifically oat milk and fresh mint."

"What do you need me here for?" Holly asked.

"I need you to keep an eye on the twins. They can't know what I'm up to. If they do, they'll ruin everything. I just know they will." Icelyn twisted her hands together. "You can use Ember to send messages to me."

"What about me?" Tasha's eyes sparkled with excitement.

"I need you to delay the event. Maybe. I might make it in time. But only if everything comes together perfectly. Plus, I need everyone to taste test the hot cocoa to make sure it's good." She wiped her hands on her apron. "I just don't want to miss out because I took too long to make up my mind, to realize not only can I have it all, but I deserve to have it all, or at least fight to have it all."

Everyone gathered around her and engulfed her in the most touching group hug ever before taking off on their tasks.

"Ember, before you go, can you light the fire?" Icelyn asked as everyone filed out the door.

The little dragon lit the fire before taking off and following Holly out the door.

Icelyn went to the kitchen area and took a deep breath before gathering a mixture of different chocolates. Her favorite cocoa to use with mint was dark chocolate, so she grabbed her favorite rich chocolate bar and started cutting it into pieces before grinding it into a powder that would melt quickly in the oat milk. She added a touch of sugar to the mixture just to ensure it wasn't too bitter. She knew that for this to work, it would have to be a perfectly balanced cup of cocoa, not too sweet, not too bitter, and not too minty. It had to be just right.

"I found them! Here are all the ingredients you asked for!" Douglas exclaimed as he burst through the door. "I don't know how you knew it would be difficult, but man, was it ever? I had to get stuff from the castle's kitchen because the grocers here were sold out."

Icelyn glanced up from her measuring. "That doesn't surprise me. I bet Maude had the twins buy everyone out. She knows this is my specialty."

"What is wrong with them? I've never seen anyone as petty as they are. It's disappointing that they live here in Wynterfell," Douglas said as he put the ingredients on the counter.

Icelyn sighed. "I don't know. But they've always taken great joy in making sure that I'm unhappy. Thinking back, it's quite unsettling."

She took her pre-measured cocoa powder, grabbed a few sprigs of mint, and threw them into the pot. That's when she noticed Douglas rocking back and forth on his feet, looking like he was seconds away from darting out, if he had permission.

"I'm sure you have better things to do than babysit me. Why don't you go take care of those? I'll be fine, and if I'm not, Ember will let you know."

"Are you sure? I can help."

"I'm sure you'll just get in my way. Just make sure when I'm running to the competition, no one gets in my way."

Douglas bowed. "Will do, milady."

She shooed him out, then turned back to her pots and ingredients. Taking a deep breath, she filled her lungs with all the smells of a kitchen—her kitchen—the scent of sugar, vanilla, and chocolate mixed together. The mint joined the mix of scents in the air as it steeped into the oat milk. She carefully strained it out, doing her best not to spill a drop of the boiling liquid. She added a dash of vanilla bean to the mixture and then slowly stirred in the chocolate, tasting it as she went until the mixture was warm, cozy, and refreshing. Once it reached the perfect melding of flavors, she stopped stirring in chocolate.

She grabbed a jar of sugar and threw a sprig of mint into the jar. Glancing over at the clock, she gasped. She wasn't going to make it unless she left right now. Hopefully, Tasha was able to delay the competition.

Chapter Thirty-Three

"Prince Colden, can I have a moment of your time?" Tasha tapped her pen on her notebook. "I would love to ask some questions before the competition starts about what today means to you."

"Now's really not the right time. We should be starting," Colden said.

"I think that makes this the perfect time." Tasha grabbed the prince by the arm, only to let go as a guard gave her the nastiest look. "I promise it won't take long."

He peeked out at the crowd, all waiting for him to start taste testing while he huddled backstage wishing this thing was almost over. There were so many different cocoas to drink, and he wasn't sure if he was actually up to the task. He had hoped that Icelyn would show up, that she would be a member of the crowd and tell him to stop this foolishness. Or better yet, that she would enter the competition and win. Just her entering would indicate she didn't mean what she wrote in the letter. But she was nowhere in sight. Colden's shoulders drooped.

"Don't look so down, Your Highness," Douglas said as he walked backstage, away from the contestants.

"What's there to look happy about?"

"Remember yesterday I told you to do whatever I said without asking questions? Now is one of those times. Go get interviewed. I will tell the crowd there's been a delay in the start of the competition."

"I can't . . ."

"Yes, you can, Colden. Now go. It's really not that hard to listen to a good friend who's trying to help you out."

"Let me make the announcement," Colden said.

"Fine, do it your way. Just delay for as long as you can."

"I think I will."

Colden made his way onto the makeshift stage that had been built in the town square. It was strange to think that a lot of what he was looking at would be gone in just a matter of days. Built solely for the festival and then demolished.

He hoped the building materials were saved somewhere. No use in cutting down more trees every year for an event this size. Maybe if the event grew, but not for a new build.

He stood in the middle of the stage. "I want to thank everyone here for making this festival one of the best Snow Solstice Festivals Wynterfell has ever experienced." He stopped as the crowd cheered. The thumping of gloved hands was a contrast from the clapping he heard at every other festival. "I am sorry to announce that there is going to be a slight delay in the start of the competition. It's my fault, I forgot that I had scheduled an interview at this time. So, I must finish the interview before I can taste all your lovely drinks without any distractions.

"But before I do, I was curious as to what happens to all the building materials used for the festival each year. Are they saved somewhere? Do we start afresh every year? Can we store them somewhere safe this year so they can be used again next year? Think about that while I go finish my interview."

Colden stepped offstage. "Is anyone going to tell me what this is about?"

Tasha and Douglas looked at each other and back at Colden, shaking their heads.

"Fine, but I'm going for a walk. I have no interest in sitting down for an interview today. At least not right now. If the crowd gets rowdy, offer them free snacks. Free food almost always calms people down."

Colden walked through town towards the woods. Everyone was at the competition, so the rest of the town felt deserted. It was nice, and also not so nice, to be alone with his thoughts; that was, until his thoughts turned back to Icelyn Frost, the girl that broke his heart in a letter. She didn't even have the gumption to do it in person, which wasn't really like her. He knew she was brave. She always stood up to him when they talked, which had allowed him the opportunity to think about things in a new light. It gave him the ability to make better decisions. Not that marrying someone because they made tasty hot cocoa was a good decision.

He could still remember how drinking the hot cocoa made him feel. It felt like someone seeing everything about a person, even all their faults, and loving that person anyway. It felt like a first kiss, a warm hug, a happy relaxing day, a day curling up by the fire with a good book. It felt like starting a new adventure and also coming home. He didn't understand it, but it was there. Many of those things he felt when he was with Icelyn. Especially the last one. Every moment around her felt like a brand-new adventure and the moment he walked through the door to his home.

He sat on the bench where he and Icelyn had sat the very first time they had met. It was like he could still feel her sitting next to him, telling him what it was like to be a shop owner in town, and how the winter festival helped shop owners, and that they still had to make enough to run both their shop and their booth. She had given him ideas to make this festival and future festivals better.

Colden stood and continued his walk through the woods, reminiscing like a lovesick puppy over the times he had spent with Icelyn, from the walks they had taken together to the carriage ride that had ended on such a bad note. He remembered the purple dragon . . .

He shook his head. This wasn't a memory of Ember; it really was Ember, and she was flying towards the competition. Why would Icelyn's dragon fly towards the competition? He followed her as stealthily as he could, hoping she didn't notice. He waited outside the contestant area as Ember slowed down and landed in front of someone. He strained his neck to see who it was. Whoever stood there was petite. He didn't think Icelyn was that short. Then, out from behind the other members of the crowd, popped a curl of red hair. Disappointment struck him as he realized Ember was spending time with Holly. Definitely not the person he wanted to see standing there. His shoulders sagged as he walked backstage.

"She's not here, Douglas," he said. "If she hadn't written the letter, don't you think she would be here?"

"Maybe . . . maybe not." Douglas shrugged. "She's had a lot going on this past week, and not all of it is good. Maybe she's still asleep. Or maybe she's careening down the street in her cart trying to get here before the competition starts." Douglas glanced over Colden's shoulder and grimaced.

"What? What is it?" Colden asked as he strained to see whatever it was that Douglas was looking at so intently.

"It's nothing, just someone driving their cart a bit recklessly. Good thing everyone else is already here. Wouldn't want anyone to get hurt." Douglas put his arm around Colden's shoulder and escorted him to the backstage entrance.

Colden looked at Douglas's hand and then back at his friend as he shrugged off his friend's arm. "What has gotten into you today? You're acting strange."

"I don't know, just excited to catch the twins and put the fear of the gods into them." Douglas rubbed his hands together and smiled wickedly. "I think it's time to get this thing started. Get up there, charm the crowd like only you can."

Douglas pushed him onto the stage, causing Colden to trip. He glared back at his guard before pasting a smile onto his face and waving. The cheering of his people normally warmed his heart, but today it fell flat. He only wanted to have one person here, and that wasn't going to happen. He did see the twins. Stacey looked positively giddy waiting at the end of the line with other competitors in front of her. All of them chatted, excited for the competition to start. Except for her brother; Dru was sneering as usual. He never looked approachable, but he did have his own insulated container of hot cocoa.

"Thank you, everyone, for coming to our annual hot cocoa competition, the last official event of the festival." He paused for the crowd's enthusiastic cheers. "Yes, the bonfire is still happening tonight as planned, so get out your marshmallows and graham crackers for a night of fun under the stars."

The crowd was eager to start. He could feel their energy. And the energy of the contestants was even higher. Someone in the crowd shouted, "Let's get this thing started already." He tried to find the person that shouted, but instead found Maude glaring at him from the front row. She was clearly there to watch over him. Maybe to make sure everything went according to her plan. Which was unlikely to happen if he had anything to say about it.

"Without any further ado, let's get the competition started." He sat down at the judging table with Douglas, Oliver, and his father. Tasha stood behind them, taking notes on everything that happened during the competition.

Chapter Thirty-Four

Icelyn dashed around her kitchen, making sure she had everything she needed for the competition. She stood back and looked at the things in her cart. She had her mint sugar, hand-warmer mugs, extra ingredients just in case, and her pot of cocoa. She couldn't find her insulated container, so she hoped the lidded pot would keep everything safe and warm. Tossing some other ingredients into a bag, she looked around one last time before grabbing the pot and heading out the door. She thought about locking the door, but her hands were full. Shaking her head with a laugh, she asked herself, *What is the point?* There wasn't really anything left to take now, anyway.

It felt like loading the cart took an extra-long time as she carefully set the pot down on the floor, trying to avoid spilling any of the hot liquid. She threw her bag in and leapt into the seat and was off. No one was on the streets in town, which was a good thing for both her and them as she careened down the street, reins in one hand, and the other desperately trying to keep the lid tight on the pot. Her pastel hair flew in every direction, every now and then blinding her to the road.

She parked her cart right at the entrance to the hot cocoa competition. Jumping down, she ran around the cart, grabbed her bag of extras and the pot of liquid cocoa. The years she had spent at Mother Maude's carrying trays back and forth to the kitchen had prepared her for this walk to the end of the contestant line. She put one foot in front of the other, feeling the ground for anything uneven that could trip her before transferring her weight. It was going great until she saw Maude.

Icelyn stopped immediately; she did not want to walk in front of her stepmother. She looked around to see if there was another path to the competition line, a way that avoided Maude. There wasn't.

"Icelyn, is that you?" The prince stood, momentarily halting the competition. He walked around the table to the edge of the stage. The crowd took it all in, their gaze starting with the prince, and then they turned to look at her. Icelyn rolled her shoulders back. There was no way Maude would do something with all these people watching. She progressed through the crowd one step at a time. She was almost directly in front of Maude when she saw the woman kick out her foot. Icelyn tried to avoid it, but Maude had perfect timing. Icelyn's foot caught on Maude's. She lurched forward, losing her hold on the lid of the pot, and warm chocolate liquid flew through the air. Icelyn stumbled but regained her balance just in time to see her mixture for the competition cover the prince. She dropped the pot as her jaw dropped in shock, covering her mouth to stop the laughter that was bubbling up. It was either laugh or cry. Neither seemed appropriate as she looked at Colden, who had hot cocoa dripping from his hair and down his face. She watched as he licked his lips, and his eyes went wide.

Colden stepped forward, covered in cocoa. "There is going to be a short break in the competition while I clean myself up. Anyone who plans on entering must have their cocoa ready by the time I return."

"But that's not fair." Dru stomped. "Stacey was the last competitor in line. Until she showed up."

He pointed at Icelyn. "She was late, but now she has time to remake the cocoa and she's going to get to enter the competition."

"You can thank your mother for that. I wouldn't need to clean up if she hadn't tripped Icelyn."

"Why I would never . . .," Maude started.

"Save it. I'm not the only witness to what you did. Now you have to live with the consequences." The prince looked over at Icelyn and nodded as he turned and left the stage.

Icelyn jumped onto the stage, Ember claiming her spot next to her. She turned to the crowd. "Hi . . . I was ready to enter the competition until, well, you saw what happened. I packed up some backup ingredients. I have my cocoa and some mint sugar. But I'm missing a couple of other ingredients. Like milk, preferably oat milk, and mint leaves. Is there anyone that can help me so I can enter the contest?"

She watched as the townsfolk looked at each other and murmured among themselves. It had been worth a try, but it didn't look like anyone was going to offer help. She sighed. Maybe Holly could run to the store while she figured out the rest.

"Why would anyone want to help you?" Maude's snide tone washed over Icelyn.

"Why would anyone want to help me? That's the question at hand. How about because I've been serving the town and the festival hot cocoa all week. People here have been able to see me, get to know me, because I have been there to serve them, figure out their favorites. I've let them know I care. Have you ever done that, Maude?"

Maude tried to put words together but was unable to string the sounds into something coherent. Her face turned bright red as Icelyn stood there staring her down.

Out of the crowd, a male voice broke through the stare down. "If you keep my favorites on the menu, I think I have some oat milk for you, if that's okay?"

"How could I say no to my best and most loyal customer at this festival?" She laughed. "Now go. Quick, before the prince changes and the competition starts."

Danny took off in a run to get the needed item.

"Anyone else able to help? I really need some mint to finish it off." Her eyes swept over the over the crowd, pleading with her eyes that someone would step forward.

"I have some mint at the apothecary. Do you want fresh or dried?"

"Fresh, please." She clapped her hands together. She couldn't believe this was going to work. All she had to do was focus on her and her abilities.

Chapter Thirty-Five

With Holly's help, Icelyn set up a makeshift table to make her hot cocoa. It wasn't much, but it would have to do the trick. She didn't have a burner to heat anything, but she had Ember, which was even better.

She dug around in her bag and pulled out the mugs, her mint sugar, and the cocoa powder she had made earlier in the day. She tapped her fingers on the table, waiting for Danny and the apothecary to return with the necessary ingredients. Ember circled around her several times before settling down underneath the makeshift table.

"Mother, what were you thinking? I had this. But now she's going to get to enter, and it sounds like we are making the same thing," Stacey whined, her voice reaching an octave rarely made by humans.

"I was thinking of how I could ensure my daughter would be queen." Maude sniffed.

"That's not going to happen now, is it? He's already dating her." Stacey jabbed her finger towards Icelyn. "And now I'm competing against her. He's going to pick her."

Icelyn couldn't help but laugh at Stacey's dramatics. She tried to ignore it and focus, but it was hard to do since everyone could hear her, and Icelyn was still waiting for her ingredients.

"Keep your voice down. You know her secret recipe, so you still have a shot," Maude whispered loudly.

"I knew it was you," Icelyn muttered. It should have felt good to know for sure who had been making her life miserable. Instead, she was sad, and angry, but mostly sad that these people who raised her disliked her so much they would put her through all of this, that they would destroy and steal her things, that they would even kidnap her. Her friends were right, she needed to stop thinking of them as family. Apparently, they were more like her archenemies.

"I got it, Icelyn. It isn't much, but it should make enough for the judges to all have a mug." Danny ran to the table she stood at, waving the milk around.

She saw Maude make a move to stop him. There was no way Icelyn was going to let that happen. Icelyn jumped down from the stage and ran towards Danny. Stopping right in front of Maude, she also accidentally stepped on Maude's extended foot. At least, she would always claim it was an accident. It's not like she would ever feel any glee watching Maude jump around on one foot while trying to hold the other. No, that wasn't like her at all.

"You did that on purpose, you little . . .," Maude said between clenched teeth.

"Did I do something? I'm so sorry if I did. I was just trying to get to my oat milk and make sure nothing happened to it or anyone trying to help me." She smiled innocently.

Icelyn could feel Maude glaring at her, almost as if her dress had caught fire in two spots between her shoulders. She knew it hadn't, though; it was just her stepmother's anger at being bested . . . again.

"Thank you, Danny. You're a lifesaver." Icelyn took the milk from him and carried it to her table on stage. "Ember, sweetie, it's time to wake up. I need your help. I need you to warm up the milk, but be careful it doesn't get too hot; we don't want it to burn."

Ember nodded very slowly. She jumped up on the table and contemplated the pot. The little dragon glanced back at Icelyn for reassurance. She nodded. Ember blew a very small stream of fire. She sure did love her dragon and thought how much she'd be lost without her.

"I have the mint here." The apothecary wheezed as he made his way towards Icelyn.

Once again, she jumped off the stage, leaving Ember with her task of heating up the milk. "Thank you, good sir. I appreciate your help. Please stop by my café when this is over. I have lots of delicious things and will set something aside for you."

She took the mint leaves from the apothecary and turned, heading back to the stage. She made her way through the crowd, knocking Dru out of the path as she did so. He stumbled and started to say something, but she (accidentally, of course) ran into him again in just the right way to knock the wind out of him. She left him there, gasping for air. At least he wasn't yelling at her and accusing her of shenanigans.

Icelyn tore the mint leaves apart, releasing their oils, and dropped them into the warm oat milk, stirring the mixture for a bit before adding her cocoa mix, and then watched the white milk become a rich chocolate color. She let everything meld together while Ember held the temperature constant for her. While the mixture finished, she dipped her mug rims in the mint sugar and set them out near the pot. She reached into her bag and grabbed the strainer. One quick sniff of the pot of chocolate and she knew it was perfect. Icelyn wiggled her fingers over the mixture. She strained the cocoa into each of the mugs. Then gave Ember a giant hug.

She carefully carried two mugs of cocoa up to the empty judging table, placing a mug in front of each of the empty judging chairs and next to the ones Stacey had already placed on the table. Holly followed behind her with two more mugs, placing them in front of the two other empty chairs. Icelyn quickly scribbled a description of her cocoa and the mug it was in onto the entry card and handed it to Tasha, leaving the stage mere moments before Douglas, Colden, Oliver, and the king walked out from backstage and took their places at the judging table.

"It appears the last entries are ready to be judged," Colden said as soon as he stepped foot on the stage. It felt like he had postponed the event until her hot cocoa was finished. The thought made her heart flutter and woke up the other butterflies that had been dormant for a while. He looked handsome cleaned up from the hot cocoa catastrophe. His icy-blue doublet brought out his blue eyes and contrasted with his dark hair.

Colden picked up Stacey's mug. He smelled the aroma wafting from the mug. He took a sip, letting the cocoa roll around in his mouth. He set down the mug. His father, Oliver, and Douglas each did the same. They reached for a notepad and made notes before moving on to her hot cocoa. She watched as Colden went through the steps with her cocoa. She couldn't read any emotions on his face. She waited for him to say something, anything that would give her a hint as to who the winner of the competition was.

Colden leaned over to discuss things with the other members of the table. Their four heads together would forever be burned into her brain. They made their decision and Colden asked Tasha for the entry cards.

The prince stood and cleared his throat. Icelyn held her breath, waiting for him to speak.

Chapter Thirty-Six

"Despite the similarities in the two beverages—it almost tasted like they came from the same recipe—one stood out above the other. It had that little extra magic you want to experience when drinking hot cocoa. So, without further ado, the winner is . . ." Colden paused for dramatic effect. "Icelyn Frost!"

The crowd went wild with its applause. Everyone stood, clapping and stomping their feet. He looked around, amazed at how excited everyone was with his pick. It seemed she had really made an impact this last week during the festival. He looked up at his winner. Tears filled her eyes, but she was all smiles. He assumed those were happy tears. He strode over to her with the prize ribbon.

"It was you this entire time," he whispered in her ear.

Her eyes widened and her jaw dropped. "Me? This entire time?"

"Yes, you," he said again. "You're behind the magical hot cocoa, the cocoa I drank and that caused me to fall in love with the person who made it because of the feelings I had while drinking it. All along, it was you."

"Are you mad no one told you?" She bit her lip, unsure of how he was going to respond to this revelation.

"How can I be mad? I've been torn since we met. I was falling in love with you and whoever made the cocoa. I thought I had to make a choice, give up on one. And this entire time it's been you." He smiled. His arms circled around her; he pulled her close. He lowered his head.

"This competition is fixed. There's no way her hot cocoa was better than mine." Stacey huffed, crossing her arms over her chest.

"Stacey, now might be a good time to back away quietly," Dru whispered. "You know, before anyone figures it out."

Douglas stepped out from behind the table and clapped Dru on the shoulder. "Figures what out, my friend."

Dru looked at the hand on his shoulder and then at Douglas. "Nothing, nothing at all," his voice squeaked.

"Good. I would hate to think that there were any shenanigans going on that I would have to take care of. Like sabotaging someone's place of business."

Colden's cheek twitched as he tried to hold back his smile. It felt good to watch Dru squirm for once.

Dru gulped. "I don't know what you mean. I'm an upstanding citizen and would never involve myself in something so sordid."

Icelyn's eyes darted between Douglas and Dru. Something was going down, and for the first time, she was ready to see it all. She was ready to see Dru and Stacey get what was coming to them.

"Dru, come on, why should I be quiet? It's not like I did anything wrong," Stacey whined.

"Oh really? You didn't do anything wrong?" Dru said, his tone dripping with sarcasm.

"Not today. Today I just made peppermint hot cocoa for the contest."

"And is that what you normally would have made, my dear sister?"

"No, I would have made something a bit more basic. But you and mother told me to make this one." Stacey pouted.

"And where did you get the recipe?" Dru asked. Apparently sabotaging Icelyn was no longer enough, but sabotaging Stacey was starting.

"Um . . . Dru . . . I don't think we should talk about that." Stacey's eyes darted around the room as she finally realized what her brother was trying to do.

"Oh, you don't think we should talk about the many times we broke into Icelyn's café and took things from her? You don't think that's a good idea," Dru screeched. Any form of self-preservation Dru ever had was gone. They lost, and there was nothing to show for all the nefarious deeds they had carried out.

Colden watched as the two siblings fought, Dru bringing Stacey down with him. He almost wanted to stop him, but the show was way too entertaining. He felt Icelyn try to take a step forward. He assumed it was to stop them, but they weren't worth her time or her loyalty. If Dru wanted to bring them down, let him. He sat back down to let the show in front of him play out.

Wait, what was Ember doing going through Stacey's bag?

"What is Ember doing? I have to stop her." Icelyn's concern was more than apparent.

Ember dug around even deeper into Stacey's bag until all a person could see were two little dragon feet kicking rhythmically. The feet disappeared and Ember's head popped out of the bag. She let out a puff of steam as she climbed out.

"What do you have there, Ember?" Icelyn asked.

Ember looked at Icelyn and tapped her toes in an excited dance. But the little dragon flapped her wings, went right by her, and flew into Colden's lap. There she dropped a book that looked well-loved.

Colden looked at the book. He carefully picked it up and thumbed through it. Inside the book were sketches of different hot cocoa drinks and pastries. Next to the drawings were recipes. Things he recognized that Douglas had brought to him during the festival.

"This looks like it belongs to you." Colden handed the book to Icelyn.

She hugged it close to her chest, her eyes filled with tears. "It's my mother's recipe book. It's my memories of cooking with her that inspired me to open my café. I thought this was gone forever."

Ember tap danced in front of her, clearly happy she had found the missing recipe book.

"Wait, stop her!" Douglas yelled. He pointed to Stacey as she attempted to sneak away from the stage.

Two guards stepped in front of Stacey. She turned to run out another exit, but all were blocked. Her shoulders drooped as she turned towards Colden. She had clearly given up. She was escorted back to the stage.

"How did this get into your purse?" Colden asked, pointing to the recipe book.

"It was all Dru's idea." Stacey pointed to her brother.

"How dare you, Stacey?" Dru's shrill voice pierced the air. "Where's the loyalty?"

"You always blame me for everything and never think I can do anything on my own. I didn't need the recipe book. I could have made cocoa without it. Now look what's happened." Stacey stomped her foot. "If I'm going down, I'm not going alone."

Colden gestured to Douglas, who came up behind the arguing twins and escorted them away.

Chapter Thirty-Seven

It had been a week since the hot cocoa competition. Icelyn stood in front of her café, taking it in again, yet somehow it felt like the first time. She read the sign: ICELYN FROST, PURVEYOR OF ALL THINGS CHOCOLATE. She was so proud of herself. She had finally done it. Her dream café was open, and after making cocoa for the festival and winning the hot cocoa competition, she had a steady flow of regular customers.

She turned towards her father as he stood next to her looking up at her café. She could see the pride in his eyes.

"I can't believe you did all this without telling me." He waved his arm toward the café. "You know I would have helped you out, sweetie."

"You have so much on your plate, I didn't want to burden you."

"You have never been a burden. At least not to me." A look of deep sadness passed over his face. "I'm so sorry I left you with such terrible people."

Icelyn waved her hand, as if doing so could erase the past. "It's done and over. We've left Maude and the twins behind. It's time for us to move forward."

She threw her arms around her father in a giant hug. She felt him let out a shaky breath as his arms circled around her. They stood like that for a few moments before letting go and stepping back to once again admire her café.

She heard the crunch of boots behind her and turned to see Holly walking arm-in-arm with Douglas. The two of them had been essential in helping her make this place a success. Their support meant the world to her. Douglas had done everything in his power to make sure she had access to the ingredients necessary to make anything she wanted. And Holly, well, Holly was her constant cheerleader. It was a necessary position, especially with all the things that had happened during the festival. Everyone needed a friend who was willing to lose sleep for them on a regular basis. That friend for Icelyn was Holly.

Icelyn felt a pair of arms wrap around her, and she took a deep breath of the wintery scent she knew went with those arms. She turned into the prince's embrace and smiled up at him. Her eyes sparkled with happiness. She stood on her tiptoes and pressed her lips against his. When she felt his smile under her mouth, her tongue darted out, an invitation for a deeper kiss. He quickly complied with her unspoken request. Unfortunately, he broke it off way too soon for her taste.

"Icelyn, we really need to talk. It's been a week since the competition, and I need to let the town know what's going on." He took her by the hand and led her into the woods where they had met for the first time.

She remembered the bench where they had sat and talked for an entire afternoon that first day. Colden gestured for her to sit, so she did. However, she wasn't sure if she was ready for this conversation. It had seemed like a good idea to enter the competition, prove that she could win it, but now—now she was supposed to marry the prince and someday become queen. She wasn't sure she wanted any of that. What she did know was she wanted to continue to work at her café and see it grow into something truly successful. It seemed impossible to believe she could have both.

"Colden, I don't know what to say. I know what I'm supposed to do," Icelyn started.

"But you don't want to . . .," he said, his shoulders slumping, as if he had already been rejected.

"It's not that I don't want to. In fact, part of me does. Despite everything, or maybe because of it, I've fallen in love with you." She looked away from him towards the trees covered in snow and ice, but her brain barely registered the beauty that was around her.

"Does that mean you want to move forward?" Excitement crept into his voice. He was unwilling, or unable, to let her finish what she needed to say.

"I didn't say that either. In a perfect world, I would marry you. I could have my café, and you could perform your royal duties. But that's not how this world works. I can't marry royalty and not have the responsibility of being royal. And I fear that those responsibilities will prevent me from following my dreams."

"I would never ask you to give up your dreams. Especially your café," Colden said. He reached for her hand.

She turned towards him. "How can you not ask that of me?"

He pushed a strand of her pastel hair from her cheek. "I love you, and I would never take away something you loved as a requirement for us to be together. The nice thing about being king and queen is that we get to make the rules. Which is exactly what we will do."

"How can you . . . we just change the rules to be together?"

"I'm a prince. It's what we do?" Colden kneeled in front of her, taking both of her hands into his.

"Oh, you're really doing this? Here? Right now?" Her eyes darted around.

"I am going to do this. But there's no need to panic. I've already talked to my father, and he's agreed that you should keep your café. He thinks it will be good to connect with the people—to reinforce our connection to the town. You will also inspire young girls to own businesses, not just be a role model as queen but also as something women can relate to. It's a fantastic opportunity."

"It seems like you've thought of everything," Icelyn said. She looked at Colden expectantly.

He threw his head back and laughed. "Icelyn, I know I've only known you for a short time, but I can't remember a time when you weren't there. Which is why you would make me the happiest of men if you would do me the honor of spending the rest of our lives together." He reached into his pocket and pulled out a beautiful ring with a stone that looked as if her mother's magic had been trapped inside it.

"Of course, I'll marry you, but I want a long engagement." Her smile was so big and bright it was magical. "Now, let's go back to the café. I'm sure I have customers waiting."

Colden removed the glove from her hand and slipped the ring on before grabbing said hand and dragging her back to the café.

"She said yes!" he hollered as they turned the corner.

The crowd that was lined up waiting to be let into the café erupted in cheers.

"For the love of hot cocoa, please say you're still going to open the café today."

Acknowledgments

Writing is both a solitary activity and yet it also takes a village. I know I wouldn't have been able to write my first book, much less the three others that have followed without the help of my family and friends. I want to thank my mom for continually taking craft classes (including a class on cozy fantasy because I was writing one). The discussions we have about the classes she takes definitely make me a better writer, even if I don't always want to admit it.

Next up, for this book especially, has to be Jamie Dalton, I honestly don't know what I would do sometimes without our Messenger conversations. Whether she's talking about what she's doing next for marketing (and I'm trying to remember it all so I can do something similar) or it's sharing plot ideas or finding new artists for covers and character art. Her positive attitude and genuine love of supporting people is amazing.

Then there's my friend Charlotte, who has read many a late night plot lines or character arcs through text. And even though she doesn't always like how I decide to spell names, she's always super supportive in helping me figure out what needs to happen next in a book, including whether or not there should be dragons. Not all friends would understand that at all times I have story ideas running through my head, which are distracting at times. But she does, and doesn't mind my "What if . . . moments.

I can't forget my friend Kat, the best cheerleader a person can have. And having a cheerleader is a necessity. She may not be much of a reader, but her support is always there in the best ways. A solid block for the imposter syndrome that creeps in.

And of course there's my dad, who doesn't know much about this book, but is essential to helping me plot my mysteries. So while he wasn't in the thick of it with this one, he did build me some amazing bookshelves to house all the books I buy.

Last but not least is my editor Sarah, who took this project on last minute and helped me iron out all the kinks (not those kind) and there were a lot of them. I'm so happy to have found her and be able to keep going back to have her edit my books.

Thanks everyone for all your support, if I haven't mentioned you yet. Trust me, I will in one of my books.

About the Author

Stephanie K Clemens is known for many things: an author, photographer, dog mom, instagrammer, adventurer, teacher, lawyer, and more. When she's not sitting behind her laptop she can be found on some adventure. Most of the time it's a road trip with her two doggos, but recently it has been in the pages of a book.

To subscribe to her newsletter go to www.stephaniekclemens.com or follow her on Instagram or TikTok at @bookishstephaniek

Also By

Ladies of WACK Series

A Study in Steam

A Practicum in Perjury

A History in Horticulture - Coming Soon

Ladies of WACK Prequels

The Daring Adventures of Honoria Porter: Volume 1

Wynterfell Romances

For the Love of Hot Cocoa

Villain Rehab - Coming Soon

Fantasy Books

Stripped Away - Coming 2024

Cursed by Bandits - Coming 2024

Children's Book by S.K.Clemens

Frankie Wants to be a Sled Dog

Turn the page for a Sneak Peek at A History in Horticulture. The next book in the Ladies of WACK series.

My derriere was up in the air as I carefully placed my baby plant in the hole and carefully pushed the nutrient-rich dirt over the roots, patting it down before moving to the next spot. Justice followed me. I pointed to where I wanted the next plant to go. Georgi's pup dug a hole. I whistled and Justice stopped. I took my next sprout and put it in the fresh hole, repeating the process until I was wiping sweat from my brow. Sitting back on my feet, I took in our progress. Justice and I had accomplished a lot this morning. It felt good. Not only did I feel this sense of accomplishment, but I also felt like myself here, in the greenhouse, more than I did anywhere else. The plants never judged me or made me feel stupid or worthless, like so many people did.

"Willa, you've done so much today. I can't believe you planted so many sprouts." My dear friend Mads walked over to where I was sitting. She was elegant as always in an emerald and gold bustle gown, her black hair piled high on her head with emeralds pinned into it. I wish I could look as put together as Mads did. Instead, I was sitting in the dirt, and I probably even had dirt smeared across my face.

"It's b-b-been a good day. Justice was an immense help." I laughed as the dog ran off, probably in search of our butler, Mr. Pendrake. He was always sneaking her extra treats.

"Of course she was. Justice does enjoy digging. I think it's one of her favorite activities. I'm impressed that you were able to teach her to stop when you want her to."

"She's a sweet g-g-girl, just needs a bit of structure. She reminds me of my dog growing up. At least Justice helps me plant instead of digging up all my plants. I've had that happen a few times." I stood up, brushing the dirt off my lavender gown. My friends here at university insisted I wear more color. When I had first arrived, almost everything I owned was a shade of brown. Now it was various shades of purple and brown. I could only stray from what made me comfortable by so much.

"Have you thought about entering the flower competition? I think the hybrid you've been working on so diligently is perfect. The Horticultural Society will love it so much." Mads was always pushing me to do things. She was the oldest of four girls, and I think she was so used to encouraging them she couldn't help herself when it came to encouraging the three of us.

"I d-d-don't know Mads. It's just a flower. It's really not that special." I brushed off her encouragement. I wasn't good at being the center of attention, and presenting my flower at the Horticultural Society would put me front and center. Besides, Lady Corinne always won, and my friends had had enough problems with her. I was sure entering the competition would only cause more trouble.

"I wish you could see your work through our eyes. Come look at it." Mads tugged me to over to where my flower was growing. I called it the Aurora because it looked like a sunrise.

"It's a nice flower. I c-c-can see that. It's why I have them throughout our house."

"It looks like a fluffy tulip that was painted by the sun. I don't know if fluffy is the right word for it, but there are just so many more petals than a tulip usually has, so it is softer in appearance, but the colors are just as vivid. I love how the tips are this deep pink color and how it fades to a pale yellow. It's spectacular." Mads watched me as she described what was right in front of me. I had worked really hard on finding the perfect techniques for cross pollinating to create this colorful hybrid. Maybe I was underestimating it. I stared at it a little longer while Mads watched me think with bated breath.

"F-f-fine, I'll enter the competition," I said with a sigh.

"Fantastic!" Mads said with glee. "Now come on, you have to get ready for your salon. You can't teach with dirt stains on your dress."

I looked down at my lavender dress and noticed I had done a terrible job of wiping it off. I was definitely going to have to change before the salon.

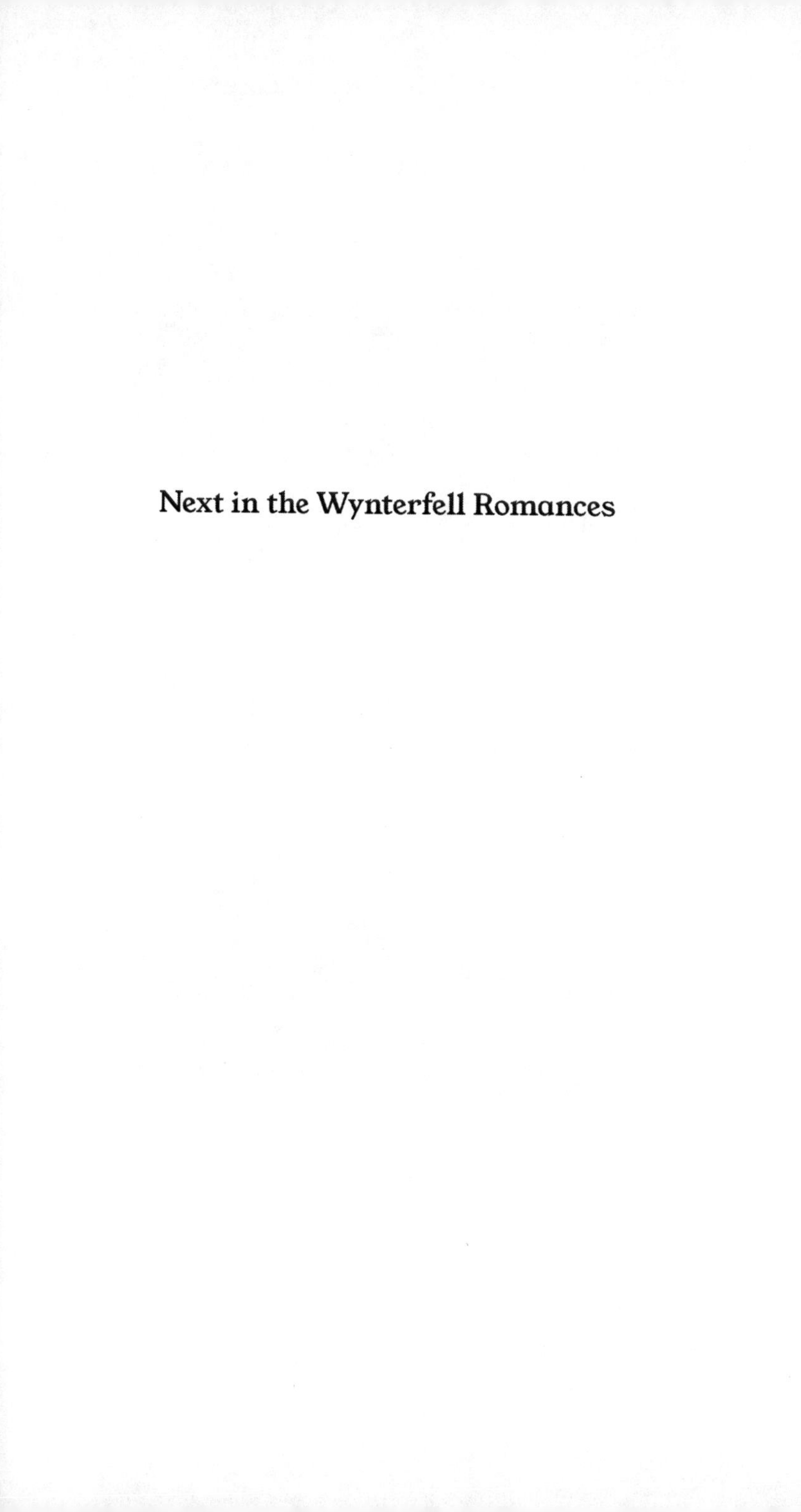

Next in the Wynterfell Romances

She Can Turn a Bad Guy Good in a Weekend.

Coming Soon

Manufactured by Amazon.ca
Acheson, AB

11329125R00179